THE GOOD THE BAD THE UGLY AND THE BEAUTIFUL

Chantelle Malone

ISBN: 0692652000
ISBN 13: 9780692652008

TABLE OF CONTENTS

ACKNOWLEDGEMENTS

First and foremost I would like to thank my Lord and Savior Jesus Christ. I have come a long way, with your help. You laid out my path, and although unsure, I followed. I put all of my trust in you, and you never led me in the wrong direction. Little did I know all the trials and tribulations I went through was all part of your master plan. I fell many, many times, but with your help I was always able to pick myself back up. My love for you is eternal. Next, I would like to thank my spiritual advisor Koffi Bessan. You opened my eyes to a lot of things. You helped me realize that there are many wonderful opportunities outside of the United States.

I would also like to thank my editor Mr. Robert Dawkins. Thank you for the endless hours you dedicated to making sure my book was edited to the best of its ability. I appreciate all of the insight and advice you have gave me. I am forever grateful to you. I want to thank my daughter Invy Bobo. I sat and read many chapters of this book to you, and you always let me know what worked and what didn't. Words can't express how much I love you. You are my motivation to achieve success to the highest level.

Next up I want to thank my public relations representative, and founder of Fat Rat productions Kenny Mcknight. You are the best at what you do. I now would like to thank someone very special in my life, Joseph Cage. We embarked on this journey together, and let me tell you I wouldn't have wanted to do this with anyone else. I want to say thank you for the countless hours I know you are going to put into marketing this book. You gave me the motivation to help me believe I could do this from day one. You were never afraid to keep me on track when I started to stray. The best part of writing this book was hearing you tell me how proud of me you were.

You believed in me at times when I questioned my own self. I will always love you Mr. Cage, and I'm 100 percent all in. I told myself I didn't want to overdue the thank-yous so I'm going to finish it up like this: If you have ever done me a favor, been a loyal friend, been a mother or father figure, been a brother or sister, encouraged me in any way, thank you. If you have ever prayed with me or for me, if you have ever disappointed me, broke my heart, or made me cry, thank you. If you have ever hurt me mentally or physically, made me feel like I wasn't worthy, made me feel ugly, or called me fat, thank you.

If you have ever made me smile, made me feel pretty, made me laugh, or made me feel special, thank you. If you have ever done any of these things to me or for me insert name here_____. I wouldn't be the woman I am today without these individuals. Whether you affected my life positively, or negatively, either way you helped me achieve something at one point in my life I thought I couldn't. I also would like to thank New York Times Best Selling Authors Ashley and Jaquavis Coleman. You both are my inspiration, and part of my success. Dad I wish you could have been here to see my success, but I know you're in heaven smiling down at me. With all of that being said, this is only the beginning for me. I'm not done yet. I have so much more I need to accomplish, so I will see you around......

Facebook......Author Chantelle Malone
Instagram......@authorchantellemalone
Email......chantellemalone@yahoo.com

FATAL MISTAKE

It was something about that particular July night. It was very quiet and tranquil. It almost seemed as if time stood still. The moon was full and reflecting off of the ocean. It appeared to be a lot more capacious than it really was. The stars were radiant that night. It seemed like they were shining a little bit brighter than usual. The breeze felt like tiny kisses on your skin. The atmosphere on the Atlantic Ocean felt too perfect, almost eerie. It was the calm before the storm. The only sound you heard out on the ocean was the waves crashing against the side of the ship.

The time was approximately 10:30pm. The Paradise cruise ship was in route to Nassau, Bahamas. The ship had departed from the Port of Miami that evening at 4:00pm. The ship had been on the water a few hours, so it was cruising at a fairly comfortable speed. The ship was due to arrive at its first offshore stop in the Birmini Islands at 0800 the next morning. Sadly, the Paradise cruise ship would never make it there, or to its intended destination.

All was quiet aboard the cruise ship. Its passengers and crew had settled in for the night. Everyone was preparing to go to sleep, and welcoming sweet dreams. Not one of them would have ever suspected that in just three and a half hours they would be living their worst nightmare. The captain however was wide awake in his living quarters. He had a strong scent of alcohol on his breath and looked rather disoriented. He grabbed the bottle of Jack Daniels from his cabinet and headed to the ship's control room.

At this time of night there was only one individual in the control room, and that was the ship's Officer of Watch. The OOW turned around when he heard the captain enter the room. "Hey captain, how's it going? We seem to be right on schedule, we may even arrive earlier than planned," he said. The captain replied back "That's great. Listen son, go get a few hours of shut eye, I will keep an eye on things down here." The OOW was a little confused. It wasn't uncommon for the captain to man the ship alone, but the captain looked a little pale. He was sweating and looked as if he was agitated by something. The OOW knew he couldn't go against the captain's orders so he shrugged his shoulders and mumbled "goodnight" to the captain and retired to his living quarters. If the OOW had known at the time what condition and mental state the captain was in that night, he would have never left him alone.

Once the captain realized he was alone in the control room, he pulled out his bottle of Jack Daniels. This was his second bottle that night, and there were no signs of him slowing down. He paced the floor of the control room. Taking sip after sip of his alcohol, the captain's mind started to wander back to why he was drinking in the first place. Only he knew that the drinking and bitterness started before the ship even left Miami. Earlier that day his wife of twenty years called him and told him that she was leaving. She then went on to tell him that her divorce lawyer would be contacting him within a week. This disappointment led him to attempting to drink away the emotional pain.

The captain then started pacing the floor in the control room, and reminiscing about all the good memories he had of his soon-to-be ex-wife. Before he knew it, he was sloppily guzzling the bottle of alcohol. Then the captain started to sob. Before he knew it he had gone into a full- fledged crying fit. The captain went on like this for about two hours. He paced the control room taking turns between guzzling the Jack and mumbling and crying under his breath. Then he started yelling "I would have taken a bullet for you Linda! I know I wasn't the greatest husband, and wasn't home often enough, but damn it, I loved you!" This was followed by another huge guzzle of alcohol and more crying. He continued on in this drunken state with his emotions transitioning from sadness, to anger to self pity.

While the captain was attempting to mend his broken heart with the bottle of Jack Daniels, he failed to realize that the currents had swayed the ship off its intended path. The ship had been cruising in the wrong direction for at least two hours. They were now cruising in unfamiliar territory. By the end of the second bottle of Jack, he would be passed out on the floor in the control room. He had come to the realization that his marriage was over. What he didn't know at the time was that his negligence would be the cause of many lives being placed in danger, and the catastrophic sinking of the Paradise cruise ship.

At approximately 0100 hours the Paradise cruise ship struck an underwater obstruction on the ocean floor. It struck the ship on its port side, tearing a gash in the bottom of the ship. The impact made a loud screeching noise underwater, and it rocked the ship violently to the left. The impact caused the captain to be thrown into a desk in the control room, waking him up. He wasn't thinking clearly when he woke up. He couldn't even remember where he was, so he ignored the disturbance and lied back down. Within seconds he was out cold again.

The movement of the ship did, however, cause Corey to wake up from his sleep. He was the captain's main watchman. He'd been working on the Paradise cruise ship since it made its maiden voyage twenty years earlier. When he felt the impact he was immediately awoken. He immediately sat up in bed. He had slept many nights on this cruise ship and was familiar with its natural sounds and movements. There was nothing familiar about the movement that he just felt. He at first decided it was nothing so he lied back down and attempted to go back to sleep. This proved to be unsuccessful. As minutes ticked by he couldn't shake the feeling of something being wrong. The feeling bothered him so much that he eventually got out of bed and headed to the control room.

The watchman opened the door to the control room and he couldn't believe what he was seeing. There, passed out on the floor with liquor bottle in hand, was the captain. The room was trashed. The chairs were overturned. The trash had been knocked over, with its contents spilled out and, it reeked of alcohol and vomit. "What the hell happened in here," Corey thought. He began pushing and poking at the captain trying to wake him. Then he began yelling "Captain Wake up! What happened in here? Who has been navigating the boat? Something rocked the side of the boat, and we need to go check the engine room! We need to make sure everything is ok!"

The captain rolled over on his back, he was still in a semi-conscious state. He started to mumble random phrases under his breath. Then Corey could hear him say "Linda, I would've given you the moon and stars. What happened, did you meet someone with a bigger cock than mine?" Corey was shocked at what he was hearing, but he knew the captain was not in his right mind. The captain seemed to be confused with his dreams, and reality. So Corey leaned down and slapped the captain hard across his right cheek. The captain's eyes popped open and he finally started to come to his senses and realize where he was. He yelled, "What the hell you do that for?" Corey replied, "Look at yourself; you were passed out on the floor. What the hell were you doing down here? Look at the navigation system. We are no longer on our intended route! We need to go check the engine room!"

They both raced down the stairs to the engine room and stood in front of the engine room door. They both were hesitant of what they would find on the other side. The captain hesitated for another few seconds; then he pushed open the heavy engine room door. What they found left them both in disbelief. The floor of the engine room was flooded with at least a foot of water, and there were gallons upon gallons still pouring in through a breach. The hole was so big, it was obviously irreparable. The captain looked over at Corey and didn't have to say a word. They both knew it was too late. The water level was rising at an alarming rate. Just within the few minutes they had been standing there, the water had started to submerge the generators and engines. Then the lights started to flicker on and off. At that moment the captain looked at Corey, and Corey looked back at him. They both knew the Paradise cruise ship was doomed.

They both stepped out of the engine room, with the captain closing the door behind them. Then they headed back upstairs to the control room. They entered the control room and Corey yelled "Captain what should we do?" The captain replied, "There is nothing we can do son. That hole in the ship is too big to repair. We can send out a distress signal to the coast guard, but they won't make it in time. I have to order an emergency evacuation. We have maybe an hour to get everyone off of this ship before it goes down, and after that may God have mercy on our souls."

Corey ran to the crews' quarters to wake the other crew members so they could prepare to release the ship's lifeboats. The captain stood in the control room alone. He began to sob as he looked around the now ill-fated ship he had run for twenty years. The ship had become his second home over the years. He couldn't believe how negligent he had been. He knew better. He was living a captain's worst nightmare. He made the decision at that moment that he would go down with the ship. He would make his grave in the Atlantic Ocean, right along side his ship. He also would go down with the guilt of knowing that he was the one that caused the disaster.

The captain walked over to the switch board in the control room. He knew he needed to make an announcement to the passengers. It pulled at his heart strings knowing that this would be the last announcement he would ever make on any ship. He knew the panic that would follow his announcement. With a heavy heart and a heavy finger he switched the intercom switch to on; he took a deep breath and began: "Ladies and gentlemen this is your captain speaking. The ship has veered off course and hit an object on the ocean floor. This has caused a rather large gash in the side of the ship that is, unfortunately, un-reparable. The ship is taking on water at an alarming rate. I need everyone to listen to the crewmembers and allow them to escort you to the upper deck in order to evacuate. We have sent a distress call to the U.S. coast guard for help, and they are on the way. Please do not panic, everything will be okay."

After the captain switched off the intercom, he went over to the control room and locked himself inside. He looked around the control room one final time, and slowly walked over to the seat in front of the control panel. He knew what was to come, and he was ready. He sat down and calmly waited for his fate. Upstairs the passengers had become panicked after the captain's announcement.

The crew members were trying their best to lower the life boats but it was extremely difficult to do in the mist of pandemonium. By the time the ship would go under, one third of these lifeboats would be occupied. The crew members were yelling at the passengers to put on their life jackets and form a line in front of the life boats, but no one was listening. The ship was in pure disarray. The people were running towards the lifeboats screaming and bawling. There were individuals being pushed to the ground. The other passengers ran right over these helpless people without stopping to help them up. All of the passengers and most of the crew members were in a panic, trying to get to the lifeboats.

By the time a few of the lifeboats were occupied the ship was lying on its side. It was going down faster than the captain had anticipated. Whoever had not made it to a lifeboat jumped overboard and prayed they wouldn't drown or die from dehydration. No one knew how long they would be stranded in the water. They could be floating for hours before help arrived. The lifeboats slowly started to drift further and further away from the ship, as it continued to sink deeper and deeper into the ocean. The life boats started drifting away from each other, spreading out in different directions.

The people in all of the lifeboats were in disbelief as to what was happening. Everyone was thinking the same thing: "How could this be happening to me?" In one of the life boats sat four women. The four woman were different in there own unique ways. Each one came from a different social background, and were complete strangers to each other. The only thing they had in common was the fact that they all decided to board the Paradise cruise ship that day, and unwittingly experience this unthinkable tragedy. Would they talk to each other, and encourage one another to think positive, or would they simply accept their fate?

These women were Jackie, Jewel, Peach, and Giselle. What were there lives like before they boarded this ship? What brought them to the Paradise cruise ship that day? If none of these ladies survived, who and what would they be leaving behind? Would they leave an honorable legacy or a questionable one? If one or all of these ladies survived, what would be the consequences of knowing they came so close to death?

JACKIE'S STORY

"What the fuck you mean you didn't make any money? You better get your ass back out there on that strip and make my money. You better not bring your ass back here again empty handed or next time I'm not gon' just slap you' I'm gon' bust your head to the white meat. Now get the fuck out my face! My daddy yelled these words at me as I quickly ran behind my house to recover the stash I had hidden there. Then I ran as fast as I could back to the diner. I made up my mind at that moment that I was never going back to that house. That would be the first and last time he would hit me.

As I continued up the street to the diner I started to think to myself, "What did I do to deserve the hand I was dealt? I'm eighteen years old, and I would give anything to live a normal teenage life." I knew that if I continued to stay in that house with my father, my life would continue to be a living hell. Unfortunately, my life had always been quite miserable. Growing up my mother and I stayed in an old run down house on the west side of town. She ran away from her parents' home when she was just thirteen years old. She was a wild teenager and had a hard time getting along with her parents. She also wasn't willing to follow the rules they had laid out for her. My mother started to spend her nights sleeping on the couches of different friends she knew from school. When there was nobody able to take her in, she simply slept on the streets.

My mother went on like this for the next three years. When she turned sixteen, you couldn't tell her she wasn't grown. Her body had developed into that of a little woman, and she had a new arrogant attitude to match it. She decided to attend a birthday party at one of the local clubs one night, and that's where she met my father. He immediately started talking sweet words in her ear and selling her a dream. He went on to tell her how fine she was, and how he loved her long black hair. He told her she had the body of a woman twice her age, and that she must have a ton of boyfriends because she was to cute not to have one.

My mother wanted to be grown, but in reality she was still young and naive. She was smiling from ear to ear and soaking up his every word. She couldn't believe this much older man was so attracted to her. She figured he had to have some money also, because as they sat there talking he ordered drink after drink, and made it clear that he would be picking up the tab. My mother had never really ventured into the act of drinking alcohol. She was having a hard time swallowing and getting use to its strong taste, but she was determined not to show it. My mother drank everything he put in front of her; she did not want him to think she was just a kid. Before she knew it the club was closing and she was extremely intoxicated from the alcohol. My father leaned over and whispered in my mom's ear. He told her, "I want to take care of you if you let me. You will never have to want for anything as long as you trust and obey me."

That night my mother sold her soul to the devil himself. She went home with him, but didn't know at the time that she had just made the biggest mistake of her life. Even though my mother was a wild teenager, she was still a virgin when she met my dad. He took my mother's virginity that night when she went home with him. She moved in with my dad, and never gave a second thought about living on the streets again or going back home to her parents. A year later she became pregnant with me.

When she told my father she was pregnant, he instantly became furious. He blamed her for allowing herself to get pregnant. He yelled at her, "What the hell were you thinking? You are old enough to know how to protect yourself from letting this happen. I don't want this baby, and I didn't ask for this baby. I don't need a baby holding me back from taking care of business, and I don't need you preoccupied with no baby. You can go get an abortion or find somewhere else to stay." My mother was petrified of my father. She also knew she didn't have anywhere else to live if he put her out. So she made up her mind to get an abortion.

Then a day or so later she changed her mind and decided to keep the baby. She went on to procrastinate day after day. Then one day my father dragged her outside to the car and he took her to the abortion clinic himself. My mother signed the papers, and my daddy paid cash for the procedure. They waited for my mom's name to be called. A few minutes later they took her back for an ultrasound and informed her that the procedure couldn't be done. She was already five and a half months pregnant. My mother started bawling as she walked back to the waiting area to confront my dad.

"What the hell you mean they can't do it?" he asked. The nice nurse who had walked my mother back to the front tried to explain to my father that she was too far into her pregnancy for them to abort, but he wasn't trying to hear anything she was saying. "Let me talk to the doctor myself!" he yelled. He got up and went to the back of the clinic peering into every room until he found the physician. The physician came out of his office and the two men started to talk. My mother couldn't hear what was going on, but she kept seeing my father pull out money from everywhere, pushing it up against the doctor's chest.

The only response we could see from the doctor was him shaking his head back and forth over and over again. Finally my dad gave up and came back to the waiting area. Everyone was looking at him in disgust when he came back to the waiting area and he knew it. He grabbed my mother's arm and practically drug her out the door. My mother was too scared to even ask him what had happened, so she stayed quiet until they returned home. Surprisingly, so did he.

Once they reached my father's house, the realization of the situation started to set in for my mother. She knew she was going to have the baby, and knew that would mean leaving my father's house. She went upstairs and started to pack her clothes in the one suitcase that she could find. She thought to herself as she packed, she was going to be living on the streets again, but this time she would be pregnant. She thought to herself that maybe she would give the baby up for adoption once it was born. She wouldn't be able to take care of it herself; she really didn't have a clue how to take care of a baby.

She thought to herself "What if I just go talk to him one more time? Maybe I can talk him into letting me stay at least until the baby is born." My mother went downstairs and found my father sitting at the kitchen table with a can of beer in his hand, and another empty can on the table. "What the hell do you want? You got us into this shit, you better figure out a way to take care of it," he told my mother. My mother took a deep breath then proceeded to talk. "Look, I'm sorry. I never meant for this to happen. If you let me stay, I promise I will do anything to make it up to you, anything at all." At first my father didn't respond, so my mother took his silence as a no. She started going back up the stairs to finish packing. Then she heard my father yell from the kitchen, "Anything, you say?" "Yes, anything," my mother said.

My father stood up from the kitchen table and went to the refrigerator and grabbed another beer. Before he sat down he looked up at my mother and said, "Okay you can stay, but don't expect me to do anything for that child when it's born. As far as I'm concerned it's your responsibility, not mine." My father then sat back down at the kitchen table and proceeded to open his third can of beer. My mother turned and walked back up the stairs. She didn't know it at the time, but once again she had sold herself to the devil.

Four months later my mother gave birth to me. My father had found and paid a phony doctor to tie my mother's tubes when I was born. He told her if she was going to be under his roof, and since she couldn't be responsible enough to protect herself, he made sure no more mistakes were made. From the time I could walk and start to put words together, I felt unwanted by my parents. I never became close to my mother or father. My mother never attempted to bond with me as a child. I was never tucked in and read a goodnight story, or given a goodnight kiss. My parents never even acknowledged my presence most of the time. My parents let it be known to me at an early age that I was just an unfortunate mistake, and they would be treating me as such.

I was also never taught to call my mother "mom." I was programmed at an early age to call my mom by her street name, "Candy." As a young child I didn't understand why, but as I got older I learned my father didn't want my mother's johns to know she had a kid. So when they heard me refer to her as Candy they assumed I was a relative and not her child. My dad took advantage of the fact that my mother would do anything for him. He started having my mother sell her body for money shortly after I was born. My mother worked the streets all night, and my father sat home and watched TV and got drunk all night. I sat alone in my bedroom a lot of the time, only coming out to go back and forth to school. I would fix myself something to eat and take it right back to my room. Every now and then my mother would come in threatening to quit walking the streets because she was tired of it, and her and my father would argue. He told her if she didn't keep bringing him his money, she could pack her things and her and I could get out. This always brought my mother to her senses and the next day she was back out on the strip.

My father's drinking started getting worse over the years. He wasn't only drinking beer, now he was drinking hard liquor as well. He then started physically abusing my mother. I'm not talking a slap here or a slap there, he would sometimes beat her unconscious, or to the point where her screaming got so loud, Mrs. Bailey, our next door neighbor, would have to call the police. My mother never pressed charges. She was too frightened of what my father might do to her.

He started requiring her to bring him more and more money for his alcohol habit. Pretty soon my mom was hardly ever at home. She stopped by the house once a day to bring my father his money and then she was back on the streets.

One night my mom came home to bring my father money and apparently he wasn't satisfied with the amount so he started beating her. I sat in my room and listened to my mother's screams. I heard what sounded like her being thrown into furniture. I heard her pleading for my father to stop, but he continued to beat her. My mother's screams got so loud I tried everything to drown out her cries. I tried turning my T.V. up as loud as it could go. Then I tried plugging my ears and humming to myself, but nothing seemed to work. I went and sat in my closet and closed the door. I sat crossed legged on my closet floor and rocked myself back and forth.

I held the pillow over my head and started daydreaming about being on a beautiful beach enjoying the warm breeze of the ocean. My daydreaming always took me away from reality and helped me to cope with my pathetic life. I always imagined swimming in the ocean, though in real life I never learned to swim. I thought of this as my own little paradise. I always promised myself if I ever had the chance to find a place like the paradise in my daydreams I was going to find a way to get there and never leave.

I had no idea how long I sat in that closet that night. It must have been awhile because I had fallen asleep in there. I came out of the closet and saw daylight. I had spent all night huddled in that small space. I immediately noticed that the screaming had stopped. I know I didn't have a good relationship with my mother, but I silently prayed that he hadn't killed her.

I slowly crept down the stairs hoping I wouldn't find my mother's body lying in the floor. I reached the bottom of the stairs and stood there for a second. I took a deep breath and turned to go in the kitchen. I didn't see anyone in there. I did, however hear my father's snoring from the other room. I reached to open the refrigerator door and my mother appeared from the downstairs bathroom. She was all dressed up. She had on a cheap tight red dress, and her good red high heeled shoes. She was wearing a pair of black shades over her eyes. There was no sun out at the time, but I was smart enough to know that she was hiding her two black eyes again. She didn't bother to cover the bruises on her arms though, as they were all up and down both of her arms. She looked up at me for a second then walked right out the door. She didn't have to say a word, I knew she was going back out to the streets.

This was my mother's life for years. She tried several times to stop selling her body for money, but every time she tried my father was there to beat some sense into her. Then when I was seventeen something horrible happened. Just when I thought my life couldn't get any worse, it did. One day when I sitting at the kitchen table and my mother was gone like always, my father came in from the liquor store. I knew he had come from the liquor store because he pulled the little brown bottle of alcohol from his jacket pocket, and put it to his lips, and took a long guzzle.

He glanced at me a second then went into his room and turned on the TV. I kept my head turned and ignored him. I sat in the kitchen and continued to make my bologna sandwich and he sat in his room and continued to drink from the bottle. A few minutes went by and I heard his cell phone ring in the other room. He started yelling and screaming and cursing into the phone. I didn't know who he was talking to on the other end but they had caused him to go off. I quickly started putting the food back into the refrigerator. I had a bad feeling something terrible had happened. My father got up out of his chair and threw his cell phone at the wall. Pieces of his cell phone went flying all over the kitchen floor. I quickly grabbed my sandwich and ran upstairs to my closet and closed the door. I sat in the closet and ate the sandwich while listening to him turn over furniture and demolish dishes. I didn't know at the time what had started this rampage, but soon enough I would find out.

Once again I stayed in that closet so long I fell asleep. I slowly came out of the closet and sat on my bed and listened. My father's rampage must've been over because I didn't hear any noise coming from downstairs. I sat in my room all morning listening and waiting, but all was silent. I decided to lie down and take a nap but as soon as my head hit the pillow I heard my father's voice. "Jackie come here!" he yelled. I laid there a few seconds and pretended not to hear him, but a few seconds later he called me again, "Jackie, come down here now!" This time he made sure he yelled it louder than he had the first time, and with a little more authority in his voice.

I immediately got a ill feeling in my stomach, and my heart started pounding in my chest. I had a bad feeling about whatever he was going to confront me about. I yelled back to him "I'm coming down! One second!" I could hear the nervous quiver in my own voice. I started taking baby steps down the hall and I got to the top of the stairs and headed down. It felt like I was in a horror film. Every step I took down the stairs was bringing me closer to my killer. Then my body became so hot I started to sweat. I'm pretty sure I was on the verge of a panic attack and I hadn't even confronted him yet. "Jackie get in here, damn it!" my father yelled again. "I'm right behind you," I responded back.

I took a deep breath and went into my parents' room. I stayed as close to the door as I possibly could. If something happened I needed to be able to make a quick escape. My father was sitting on the edge of the bed, and like always he looked discombobulated, like he had been drinking. He only had on a dirty faded pair of underpants and nothing else. He had liquor bottles strewn all over the bedroom floor, and I could smell his bad body odor from where I stood by the door. I didn't want to look directly at him so I just looked down at my feet and kept my gaze there.

"Yes," I said. He replied, "Listen here: your mother was arrested last night. She tried to sell drugs to an undercover agent. I don't have any money to bail her out, so she is going to be in jail for awhile. We are going to need some money coming in this house. You are almost eighteen now. This is a good time for you to step up and fill your mother's shoes." I stood in front of him dumbfounded and with my mouth hanging open. I didn't know what to say. I couldn't believe what I was hearing. My father wanted me to sell my body for money just like my mother.

I could not believe he would even ask me something like this. I know he didn't care or even claim me. But the reality was, like it or not, I was his blood. I was his daughter. I acted confused like I didn't know what he meant, so I replied back, "I can start looking for a job tomorrow; I will go down to the diner and see if they need any help." "You are not working in a damn diner, I need money now. You are going to get out there and take over your mother's clients. Just do what they tell you to do, and bring me my money!" he yelled in my face. "Now you better go upstairs and get yourself together. Your mother's clients are expecting you as soon as possible, so you are going out tonight."

I turned and ran out the bedroom, and ran back upstairs to my room. I started crying uncontrollably. What the hell was wrong with him? I was his daughter for Christ's sake. Did that not mean anything to him? This was an all time low even for him. At that moment I really realized that he didn't give a damn about anyone, not my mother or I. The only thing he cared about was how he was going to get money for alcohol. I felt hopeless and terrified of what lay ahead for me. I was still a virgin; I didn't want some random, disgusting John taking my innocence for fifty dollars.

I needed to get out of this house. I needed to run away, but where would I go? I had no friends, or family. I didn't know my father's family, and my mother's family had disowned her years ago. I didn't even know where they lived to locate them and beg them to help me. I began to feel depressed. I didn't have anywhere to go, and no one to turn to for help. I lay down on my bed and cried. I cried until my throat became painful, and my eyes became red and puffy.

I wished I could just die at that point. No one would care anyway. I wouldn't leave anyone behind that would grieve my passing. It would be like I never even existed. I pulled myself up off of the bed and went and sat in my closet. It always brought me comfort sitting in there. When I sat in there and daydreamed about my paradise for a few minutes, I was able to forget how miserable and depressing my life was. I shut my closet door and sat down. I closed my eyes and concentrated on my paradise.

I was always so happy when I daydreamed about my paradise. I could do whatever I wanted. There was no one there forcing me to do things I didn't want to do. It was peaceful and quiet. There was no one yelling and spitting in my face. The only noise I heard was coming from the ocean. This was the life I wanted. This was the life I needed. This was the life I deserved, and I was determined now more than ever to get there. I knew exactly where to find it. A few days ago when I was upstairs watching television in my room the weirdest thing came across the television. There was a commercial that came on advertising a cruise to the Bahamas.

The ship was stunning. The people in the commercial looked happy. What really caught my attention is where it was going. It was cruising to a place called the Bahamas. It looked sensational. It looked just like the paradise I daydreamed about all the time. It had the palm trees, and the captivating white sand. The ocean looked so beautiful it left me speechless. I couldn't believe there was a place like the one I imagined that actually existed. My eyes were glued to the commercial until it went off. I wished I could have rewinded it and watched it over and over again. At that moment I wanted to go there at all costs.

I would never come back to this house. I would never even return to the states. I would live out the rest of my days on that island. I wanted a new life. I had to get on that cruise ship, but there was one major problem holding me back. I called the eight hundred number on the commercial and they told me the cheapest ticket would cost eight hundred dollars. I had to come up with a plan, and figure out how to get the money. It wouldn't come from selling my body, that's for sure.

I sat upstairs all day and tried to brainstorm how to make some quick cash. I was still sitting in my closet when I heard my dad coming up the stairs. I quickly stood up and came out of the closet into my room. I went over and lay across my bed so he would think I was sleeping. "Jackie get your ass up and get dressed. You need to get out on the strip so you can start bringing me some money, and if you come back here empty handed, you will have hell to pay!" he yelled.

My father then turned and walked out of my room and back downstairs. I was afraid of what he would do if I stayed in the house, so I had to at least get up and leave. I got out of my bed and put on the biggest, ugliest clothes I could find. I put on some old jeans with rips in the knees. I put on an old pair of Adidas shoes with holes in the toes, and to top off my unpleasant look, I put on an oversized grey sweatshirt with an ink stain that wouldn't come out. I thought to myself that maybe if I looked unappealing the Johns would just leave me alone. I didn't care what my dad had assured them I would do; no one was going to touch me. I was not going to sell my body to some nasty, perverted man to support his drinking habit. I really needed to figure out how to make some cash now. I needed to leave that house, the quicker the better.

I left the house and headed over to Sherman Street. Sherman Street was two blocks over from the strip, where my father thought I had gone. There was a twenty-four hour diner on Sherman, so I decided I would just sit inside the diner all night and then go home in the morning. I would just tell my father that none of the Johns approached me. I sat in the diner and watched the prostitutes come in with their pimps to eat. The pimps came inside the diner first, with their three piece suits and shiny shoes. The harlots followed with their tight dresses, and painted on make-up. I noticed some of the prostitutes cut their eyes at me, and some of them looked at me like they felt sorry for me.

I sat and listened to those pimps make all kind of promises to the women, and they were hanging on their every word. Then the pimps started telling them what they wanted to do sexually to them, and they just batted their fake eyelashes and giggled. The whole situation made me sick to my stomach. Those pimps sure knew how to sell a dream. I didn't understand it. Didn't they know what they had to do for these men?" I noticed that just about everyone that came to this diner were prostitutes with their pimps. I also noticed that the pimps were so stuck on trying to maintain their image that they always left massive tips on the table.

I didn't see one dollar bill hit the tables at all; it was all tens and twenties. There were only two waiters working that night. I noticed it took them forever to come around and pick up the tips off the tables. This started me to thinking, I could easily get over to those tables and just take a few bills before they came around to clean and collect their money. I hated the idea of stealing, but I knew this might be my only chance to get some quick cash. I was scared to make a move at first for fear of being caught. I didn't know what to do.

At that moment I closed my eyes and prayed, "Lord I don't know what to do, or where to turn. My father wants me to do something incredibly horrible that I am not willing to do. I have never stolen anything from anyone in my life, but I need this money. I need to be able to leave my father's house, I'm scared of what he might do to me if I don't. Please protect me. I am trying to get away from this hell I'm living in. Please forgive me for what I am about to do. Amen."

I got up from the booth I was sitting in and headed towards the nearest table with money on it. I quickly glanced around the diner to be sure no one was looking, and then I took a twenty dollar bill from the table and stuffed it in my pocket. I quickly headed back over to my booth feeling positive that someone would yell "hey" at me. But no had even noticed me. I forgot I was wearing the big ugly clothes. I wasn't necessarily drawing attention to myself like the prostitutes were. I didn't care; it just made the task at hand easier.

The prostitutes and their pimps continued to come in all night. When they got up to leave the pimps nonchalantly dropped a few big bills on the table. I made sure I was ready to make my move as soon as they left. I never got too greedy I knew that would get me caught. So I stuck to just lifting a ten or twenty dollar bill depending on how much they left. I took a break after a few hours and went into the bathroom to count the money I had taken. I couldn't believe my eyes, in just a few hours I had lifted two hundred dollars! I was ecstatic, at this rate I could buy my ticket sooner than I thought. This actually caused me to smile, something I hadn't done in a very long time.

I left the restroom and came back into the diner. The sun was starting to come up. I had sat in here all night long. I knew I had to go back home and face my father. I started walking back home contemplating what I would tell my dad when I showed up empty handed. After all, I had witnessed what he had done to my mother when she just came up short one night. I arrived at my house and snuck into the backyard first. I hid the money I had stolen up under an old dog house we had in our back yard. I knew if my father found out I had money he would take it for sure. I quickly let the dog house back down and jogged back up to the front of the house.

I walked up the front porch and turned the knob. The door came open. The fact that the door was already open scared me to death. I stepped into the kitchen and looked around the corner into my parents' room. I was praying that he was gone. I started to walk slowly up the stairs to my room when I heard my father's voice. "Jackie, come here!" he said. He was sitting in the TV room across from my parents' room. I instantly froze. I was so panicked I couldn't speak or let alone move. I started debating whether I should go in. Should I just run back out the door? I didn't know what I should do. Then I heard my dad's footsteps coming up the stairs behind me. I was so terrified, I thought "Maybe I should just have a heart attack and die before he gets up here."

I tried to calm myself down and slowly breathe in and out, but it wasn't working. I would just tell him no one approached me. No one was interested so I didn't make any money. I heard my father reach the top of the stairs and he started walking down the hall to my room. I stood in the middle of my bedroom and waited. I had nowhere to hide, it was too late anyway. He was right outside my door. He stood outside the door for a second, and then kicked the door open. He kicked it with so much force the knob hit the wall in back of it and left a huge dent. He came into my room and the first thing I noticed was his bloodshot eyes. He had the look of a devil, like he was possessed. He was wearing dirty blue sweatpants and a mechanics work shirt. He had his shirt open and I could see the food and vomit stuck in his chest hair. He was a walking disgrace.

I wanted to run around him and try to get away from whatever he intended to do to me, but my legs wouldn't move. Then he yelled with slurred words, "Where the hell is my money Libby? How much did you make?" I slowly started backing further and further into my room. I knew my father was drunk out of his mind. He was calling me by my mother's real name. He was so intoxicated he didn't even realize he was seeing and talking to me. Then he screamed again, "Libby where the hell is my money?"

"Dad, I'm not Libby. It's me, Jackie, your daughter. I didn't make any money last night. None of mom's clients approached me," I said. I was silently praying that he would just accept my reason for not having any money and leave the room. "What the fuck you mean you didn't make any money? I set up appointments for you. You have been gone all night, and you bring your ass back here empty-handed?" he yelled. Then as quick as I could comprehend what was going on, he raised one of his huge, nasty calloused hands and slapped me across the face. The force of it knocked me off my feet and I fell to the floor.

Then the pain came. It was excruciating. I couldn't move my jaw, and my ears were ringing. I quickly started scooting away from him. When I got a safe distance away I stood up and darted around him and ran out the bedroom door. It's a good thing he was drunk and his coordination was off or he would've reached out and grabbed me. Instead he reached out and swung at the air. I ran down the stairs as fast as I could and out the front door. I ran into the back yard, grabbed my money, and ran away from that house as fast as my legs would take me. Halfway down the block I turned and looked back at the house I had grown up in. It looked just as miserable on the outside as the life I lived on the inside. I hated that house. It was a prison. It's a wonder the city had not condemned it years ago. The grass around the house was at least up to my knees. The paint on the house was two different colors, because it started peeling years ago. The blinds in all the windows were broken and missing slats. I was glad to be getting away from that hell hole. I knew I would never set foot back in that house again. I turned away and continued running.

I didn't know where I was running to at first. I didn't really know where to go so I headed towards the diner. There was no way I was going back to that house. He would probably kill me next time. I had so much hatred in my heart for my father putting his hand on me. He could die today and I wouldn't shed one tear. In fact I would spit on his grave. I knew in my heart he would never see me again. I went into the diner and took my usual seat in the booth in the back. I waited for the sun to go down, and just like clockwork the usual crowd of prostitutes and pimps started to come in. As soon as the diner got scarce and the pimps and entourages left, they made sure they dropped a nice sum of bills on the table.

There was no fear or hesitation in me this time around. When they left I quickly went to work sliding the ten and twenty dollar bills in my pocket. After a few hours I started to nod off at the table. I knew I couldn't fall asleep in the booth that just might be enough to make someone pay attention to me. I had nowhere to go, and I didn't want to stray too far away from the diner. For some reason I felt safe when I was there. I didn't know what else to do so I went into the ladies' rest room. The smell of urine hit me instantly. It was so atrocious it burned my nose. I looked around and there was tissue and used condoms laying everywhere. The mirrors were cracked and there were empty broken liquor bottles in the sink. I opened the door to one of the stalls and the toilet was overflowing.

Someone had tried to flush a pair of panty hose down the toilet. I closed the stall door and opened the next one. There was a huge puddle of blood on the floor. I covered my mouth and forced the vomit that was coming up back down. I closed that stall door and open a third. This stall wasn't too bad aside from the used condoms on the floor. I let the toilet seat down and sat on the toilet. I put two small pieces of tissue in my nose to block out some of the urine smell.

I rested my arms up on the bar in the stall, and then laid my head down on my arms and fell asleep.

I never let myself fall into a deep sleep in fear of being caught in the bathroom. I was able to take a cat nap for an hour or so and then I went back out to my booth to continue collecting money. I always had the feeling that the older waitress with the big bosom reminded me of Madea, from Tyler Perry's plays knew I was taking the money, and also sleeping in the bathroom, but she never said anything to me, and no one else did either. Everyday I was terrified my father would walk in that diner and drag me out by my hair, but thank God he never showed up. I stayed in that diner and pinched off tips for a total of four days.

On Friday of that week I bought a bus ticket to Miami, and a ticket to board the Paradise cruise ship. The ship was scheduled to leave on Saturday, so that night after I had collected a little more money, I walked six blocks to the bus terminal. I was so happy to see that Greyhound bus pull into the terminal the next morning. I got on the bus and was on my way to Miami. It felt so good to finally be leaving this hell hole. I had never been this happy in my life. I didn't know how to handle the emotions plaguing my mind. As the bus turned onto the main road to take us to the interstate, I started to cry. This time they were happy tears. I was on my way to a new life. I didn't really have a plan, I just knew when I made it to the Bahamas I was never leaving.

I couldn't believe everything I had daydreamed about was now becoming a reality. My bus ride was going to be a little over six hours long, so I decided to close my eyes and get some sleep. The little cat-naps I had been taking over the past couple of days was catching up to me. I didn't think I would sleep the whole trip, but once I closed my eyes, I didn't wake up until I felt the bus driver tapping me gently on the shoulder saying, " We are here young lady, wake up."

I quickly exited the bus and looked around outside. I didn't see the ship. I started to look around frantically from side to side. "Where is it? The ship is supposed to be right here at the dock," I thought. I wondered if the bus dropped me off at the wrong spot. Then I did a more thorough scan of my surroundings and spotted a little office that had a check-in sign above the door. I ran over to the office and knocked on the door, and a short elderly lady answered, "Can I help you sweetie?" she said. "Um, yes. I'm supposed to board the Paradise cruise ship here today, did I miss it?" I asked as I silently prayed she would say no.

"Oh no, honey you didn't miss it. It's not due to arrive for another hour. There is a diner across the street if you want to grab a bit to eat," she said. "Okay, thank you" I replied. "Thank you Lord!" I was just early and I hadn't missed the ship. I decided to wait at the diner. I quickly ran across the street to the diner and found a seat in a booth in the back. I wasn't very hungry. I was too nervous and excited to eat, so I just ordered a blueberry muffin. After a few minutes of sitting in the booth, and picking at my muffin I quickly checked the clock on the wall. The ship was due to arrive in twenty minutes. I quickly pulled out a ten dollar bill and left it on the table. I wrapped up the remainder of my muffin, stuck it in my pocket and headed out the door. As I walked out of the diner it occurred to me instead of stealing tips off a table I was now leaving a tip.

I got back across the street and no sooner than I could turn the corner I saw the ship approaching. It stopped me dead in my tracks. It was breathtaking. It was huge. It was probably three times the size of my high school football field It was even more beautiful than I had imagined. It was all white with blue trim around the windows. The ship had rows and rows of windows. I wondered, how many rooms a ship like this had. I'm sure it must be hundreds. It was everything I had daydreamed and more. I ran over to the boarding sign and waited. I wanted to make sure nothing stopped me from getting on this ship. I didn't have any luggage to bring so I would be able to get right on. I'm sure I looked like a runaway to everyone. I still had on the same stained and torn clothes I had on when I left my house, but I didn't care. This was the happiest day of my life.

After a few short minutes I was able to board the ship. The minute I stepped on that ship it felt like all my burdens had been lifted away. I know what they mean when they say it feels like the world has been lifted from your shoulders. That's exactly how I felt. I was already feeling the change within me. I felt like a new person already. I finally felt like I could start living. I wouldn't have a care in the world. I boarded and walked casually down the corridor of the ship. Everything looked and smelled flawless. There wasn't a crumb on the floor and all the lights in the corridor sparkled. I was scared to touch anything in fear of tarnishing the ship's clean décor, so I avoided coming into contact with anything as I searched for my room. I quickly found my room, scanned my card, and walked in.

The inside of the room was just as spectacular as the outside. Everything was clean and in order. The room looked like a little apartment. There was a little kitchen with a dining area attached. I even had my own bathroom with a huge tub. I couldn't wait to take a bath, and stretch out in the tub. The queen sized bed was huge compared to my twin sized bed I was had to sleep on at home. I couldn't wait to check out all the channels on the flat screen TV that came with the room. I walked over to the patio, and looked out at the ocean. I looked up at the sky and the only words that could come out were "Thank you God. Thank you for saving me." I stood there looking out at the ocean and I started to cry. For the second time in my life I was crying happy tears.

Jackie Present Day

Boom, Boom, Boom! "Ma'am wake up, wake up it's an emergency!" the crewman yelled. "The captain has ordered an emergency evacuation!" I heard banging and I jumped out of bed and started running into the direction of what I thought was my closet. I hit the wall and I immediately came to my senses. I realized that I wasn't at home. That's right, I thought to myself. I'm not at my father's house, I'm on a cruise ship. So who the heck would be knocking on the door at this hour? I stood in the middle of the room and then I heard the banging again. Boom, Boom, Boom! This time I went over to the door and asked, "Who is it? Who is out there? Can I help you?" Then a voice replied, "I'm a crewmember for the ship." I opened the door and one of the crewmembers stood there. He looked like he was in a panic. I couldn't help but wonder what was going on. "Ma'am you need to come up to the upper deck immediately. The captain has ordered an emergency evacuation effective immediately," he said.

"What! Are you serious?" I asked. "Yes ma'am, I am very serious," he replied. He stepped aside and I peeked down the hall. I saw people running around in a frantic panic. That's when I realized this was no joke; this was for real. I quickly went back in the room and put on my clothes and shoes as fast as I could. I headed down the hall trying to keep up with the man that had awakened me. He led me and a group of other people to the upper deck of the ship towards the lifeboats. Once we reached the upper deck I was in total shock.

It looked like I was standing in the middle of some kind of movie set. This couldn't be real. Everyone was in a panic. There were tons of people fighting and pushing to get to the lifeboats. I didn't know what I should do. I just did like everyone else and started making my way towards a lifeboat. I still couldn't quite process what was going on. I saw the terror on the other passengers' faces, but it just wasn't registering. It was like I was in shock and I couldn't react to what was going on.

Then, before I knew it I was practically pushed onto a lifeboat with three other women, and the lifeboat was lowered into the pitch black ocean. I had always been afraid of the dark as a kid, so when they started to lower us into the ocean I began freaking out. Everything was pitch black. There wasn't much lighting from the ship since the electricity had started to fail. The best light we had was coming from the moon in the distance. I began to become terrified. I started breathing heavily and shaking uncontrollably. I hated being in the dark. Then my fear turned to anger. After everything I had been through, how could this be happening to me? I had been stealing money and sleeping in a not so pleasantly smelling bathroom to buy a ticket on this ship. I was finally going to be free. I was finally going to be happy for once in my life. My daydreams were finally becoming a reality. Then my anger turned to hopelessness. I started to think to myself, "I should have known. I should have known it was too good to be true for something good to happen to me." I didn't know how long it would be before help would come, or if anyone was coming to rescue us at all. I did know that if we were rescued they were going to take us back to the states. But I didn't want to go back to the states. My father was looking for me by now, and I had a feeling he wouldn't stop until he found me.

I did know I was not going back to my father's house. He was not going to turn me into his punching bag and whore. I would die before I let that happen. At this point I would be okay with dying out here, if it meant I wouldn't have to face my father again. I slowly looked around at the other three women who sat in the lifeboat with me. One of the ladies was probably my mother's age. The other two were around my age. They all looked just as scared and terrified as I did.

I leaned back against the lifeboat and closed my eyes. I started to block out the sound of the crying coming from the other women, and the sound of the ocean. I started to daydream about my Paradise. I was so close to making it a reality. I just hoped and prayed that if help didn't come, we wouldn't suffer.

JEWEL'S STORY

"Here are your Prada shades ma'am. Thank you for your purchase," the store clerk said. I needed new shades and you guys always have the hottest shades in town," I replied. Some people would think I'm insane for spending five hundred dollars on sunglasses. Fortunately for me five hundred dollars was like pocket change. Everyone wasn't as fortunate as I. The nicest part about it is I haven't had to lift not one of my two hundred dollar manicured hands to work. I have never been broke a day in my life. When I was born I was put into a custom decorated nursery by Frances, a very famous interior decorator to many Hollywood celebrities.

In case you have been living under a rock all of your life, let me educate you by telling you who I am. My name is Jewel Alexander. My mother knew what she was doing when she named me. My name fits me to a tee. I'm beautiful, precious, and I don't come cheap, just like a jewel. My parents knew what kind of girl I would be, that's why they gave me this name. My parents are both very wealthy. They have old school money. They started making money before I was even born. They never really planned on having any children so you can imagine my mom's reaction when she found out she was pregnant.

She was thirty-five years old and at the peak of her medical career. Her and my father ultimately decided to keep the child, since neither of them had any siblings. They figured if something happened to them would they leave all of their assets and money to me. They wanted their legacy to live on in some form. Even though my parents ultimately decided to keep me they didn't want any more surprises. My mother decided to have her tubes tied once I was born.

In today's day and age most OB/GYN physicians would not perform such a permanent procedure on a woman with just one child, but my parents knew a lot of wealthy people who also wanted their services. It was nothing for my mother to have her friend Cynthia perform the procedure for her. Cynthia was an OB who ran her own practice uptown, and my mother had known her for years. They had been tennis partners at the country club for at least ten years now. In return, my mother performed a procedure for Cynthia. My parents were both very well known plastic surgeons. Combined they both perform over 500 procedures a piece per year. That's a lot of nips and tucks.

Being in that field, my parents knew a lot of wealthy individuals who came to them for their services. And sometimes there was no money involved. They would trade a service for a service, like my mother and Cynthia. My mom needed her tubes tied and Cynthia wanted a breast lift so an agreement was reached between the two and both parties were satisfied. They all had one thing in common. They had money. So much money they didn't know what to do with it.

My parents were workaholics. They were always at their practice. Most days they were up at 5:00 a.m. and out the door by 6:00 a.m. If there was some sort of social function or charity event going on after work, they wouldn't get home until well after midnight. Sometimes they didn't come home at all. They would stay at one of their friend's guest houses. When I was born my mother decided to hire a nanny. She didn't want to compromise her way of life. She didn't want a baby getting in the way of having a career. I remember her numerous times on the phone telling her friends that she couldn't be tied down with a child all day. "I have a practice I need to tend to." For the longest time as a young child I thought my nanny, Alma, was my mother.

I was with Alma night and day. I was lucky if I saw my real mom and dad twice a week. They tried to always make up for not physically being there by buying me numerous expensive gifts. They mostly had Alma purchase several lavish gifts for me. They always made sure that Alma inform me that the gifts were from them. When I got older and my school was having special functions or events, I always went with Alma. My teachers and what few acquaintances I had didn't know what my parents looked liked. So they all assumed Alma was my mom. My parents never physically got involved with the PTA or school fundraisers. They always made their presence known with their money. For instance, the school was selling candy bars to help raise money for new school computers. Instead of getting involved and helping me to sell the candy bars to their friends they just sent a big check to my school to cover the total cost of all new computers.

Technically, the rest of the kids didn't have to sell a single candy bar. The school loved my parents because they loved their money. Donations like this one made some of the other kids' parents upset. They didn't like the idea of my parents just giving the school money. The other parents felt like us kids needed to earn the money ourselves. I totally disagreed with them. I figured why put in all that work if you don't have to. I think most of them were just jealous of my parents' wealth. I think they didn't like the fact that the school's principal let me cut the ribbon at the opening ceremony for our new computer lab my parents paid for. Other kids wanted to know how come they couldn't be a part of that. I simply told them everybody can't be as fortunate as I am.

Okay back to Alma. She was pretty cool but she was a little strict. Alma had been with me since I was an infant. My parents hired Alma when I was just three months old. The first nanny they hired came from an online recruiting agency. My mom says she was young and seemed like she could handle the job, but she had sticky fingers. My mother's diamond jewelry started to come up missing, and so did a lot of her designer dresses and shoes. She was fired after two weeks. My mother had learned her lesson from hiring anyone online so she asked her friends at the country club for recommendations. Alma's name came up a few times from other country club members. She came highly recommended from a few women who had used her services years ago.

Alma turned out to be exactly what my mother was looking for. She was kind and always very thorough and prompt. She was clean and she followed orders to the tee. That's what really won my mother over because she never had to go in behind her or tell her anything twice. My mother loved the fact that Alma ran everything by her as far as my care. From my routine bedtimes to what kind of food I was being prepared.

Alma was a great stand- in parent to me. I always considered her like a second mom as I was growing up. She did all of the things a real mom would do. It wasn't just a job for Alma. She took care of me and loved me like she would her own child. Unfortunately, my mother had told me years ago that Alma loved children but she couldn't have any of her own. I'm sure that had something to do with her going into the childcare business. From the start, Alma and I got along. Every once in awhile, we had little disagreements. Like for instance, she always made sure I was in bed on time on school nights. She didn't care how much I begged or what the circumstances were. I had to be in bed on time. I had to leave many social functions as a kid because of Alma's strict bedtime rule. She wouldn't argue with me about it either she would just simply tell me "Jewel you need to get an adequate amount of sleep or you won't be able to perform at your top potential in class."

Alma, overall, was okay in my book. I couldn't help but to be nice and respectful towards her, and plus she had my credit card. When my parents hired Alma they gave her a credit card to use specifically for my needs. My parents' names were on it, but as Alma proved herself trustworthy, my mom eventually made Alma an authorized user. Alma always thought my parents spoiled me. She never questioned my mother about the things they bought me or the things they allowed me to have, but Alma sometimes told me I was "acting like a spoiled brat." I didn't think I was a brat, I just wanted things when I wanted them with no questions asked.

Alma didn't like the fact that I had to have everything that was currently in style. I couldn't stand anything outdated. I wouldn't be seen with anything outdated. This applied to my clothes, my shoes, my purses, everything. I even had to wear my hair in the newest updated styles. This caused me to have to do a lot of shopping. I felt like I shouldn't have a spending limit when it came to keeping me looking good. My parents deposited my allowance into my credit card account every month. My allowance was twenty-five thousand dollars a month. Even though I hardly ever saw my parents, they always made sure I was taken care of financially. This made me happy because I had to go shopping for new things every weekend and I would be so embarrassed if my card didn't work. Lucky for me we never had issues with money. Every month like clockwork, money was on my card.

The best was yet to come. When I turned thirteen my parents hired me a driver/bodyguard. They figured I was old enough and mature enough to do my own shopping. I was really excited because that meant I could carry my own credit card. My money was now in my possession. They also thought that Alma was getting too old to be running me around town.

Now I never really had any friends at school. Once the girls found out at school that I had a driver and my own credit card they went ballistic. They were so jealous, I almost felt sorry for them. I knew every girl in my school wished they were in my shoes, unfortunately for them they weren't. Some of my parents' friends had something to say about me. My parents didn't care. They simply ignored all the snotty comments they kept hearing about me turning into a spoiled brat. They figure they were always busy and they didn't want me interfering in their careers so they kept me happy with their money. I didn't have a problem with it.

My driver/bodyguard, JT, was really cool. He was a big man. He had to be at least 6 feet tall and 250 pounds of pure muscle. He always wore all black, and he never went anywhere without his black Ray-Ban shades on. He never complained about any-thing. No matter how many places I asked him to take me, he did with no questions asked. He was my bodyguard but he knew how to protect me while making sure he gave me personal space. He wasn't smothering. I liked the guy. I often wondered how much my parents were paying JT to look after me. I know he was just there to work for me but it was nice having someone new to talk to. I couldn't talk to my parents. I hardly saw them anyway. There were always in and out of town. Even when they were in town sometimes I didn't see them.

I tried being friends with some of the girls at school, but that didn't work out. They were always so jealous of my parents' wealth, and the things I had. They were jealous of the freedom I had as a teenager. A lot of the things I did for fun they couldn't do, or just didn't have the money. Their parents didn't have the connections my parents had. We went to several concerts together but they always got mad because I was given VIP access and allowed back stage for autographs while they had to stay out front with the common people. After hearing them complain about me leaving them behind I de-cided to just do things solo. It was better that way.

I always heard kids whispering in the hallway at school about how arrogant I was because I had money. I didn't care. The truth is I am better than them. So I figure they were just complementing me. I didn't need broke girls as friends anyway. They would never be able to keep up with my lifestyle. At the end of the day, I had all the com-panionship and happiness I wanted in my American Express credit card. It never let me down. I didn't have to worry about it using me or being disloyal to me. I couldn't say the same for the girls that were trying to be my friend.

People sometimes ask me if I wished my parents would spend more time with me, but honestly I don't know how to respond. I do sometimes I wish I had my mom around to talk to me about fashion and makeup. I also wish I had my father around to talk to me about teenage boys and their real intentions. At the end of the day, the reality is they have been popping in and out of my life for so long, I have gotten accustomed to them not being in my life.

I often think if I had been born into a normal middle class family, and not my wealthy one, there are a lot of things I would not have been able to do. I love being able to go in the store and buy whatever I want, when I want. So I ask myself, would I trade all the money and privileges I have just to have my parents in my life? Probably not. I know it sounds cruel and selfish but that's just the way it is. Life in every aspect is easier if you are wealthy. Having money in my book is like having everything. People say money can't buy happiness. If they were walking in my thirteen hundred dollar Christian Louboutin heels they would think differently.

The older I got the more freedom my parents gave me. They eventually told Alma they didn't need her to care for me anymore. Alma understood the decision my parents made. She knew I was getting older and would be grown in a few years anyway. I was a little disappointed to learn that Alma was leaving. She was the closest person to a mom I had ever had. She had taught me a lot over the years. I hated to see her go. I had become so accustomed to her being in my life. I knew Alma was a good woman with a big heart. I would truly miss her.

I knew Alma would be leaving soon, so JT and I took her out to a lavish Mexican restaurant for dinner. We also took her shopping at Macy's. Alma decided to stick around until the day after my eighteenth birthday. I knew it was going to be difficult for me to say goodbye to her. Alma had been such an intricate part of my life. That night my parents flew in from out of town to bring Alma her last paycheck and to thank her for everything she had done. We all stood in the foyer when it was time for Alma to go. Everyone took turns saying their goodbyes. My parents told her they appreciated everything she has ever done for me. They told her that if she ever needed anything to call them.

My mother then handed Alma a large brown envelope with her name on it. My mother told Alma the envelope contained her last paycheck and another little gift from her and my father. Alma looked up at my mom with confusion on her face. Then she looked over at me. I just shrugged my shoulders. I didn't know what they were doing. I was just as curious as she was. We all stood around Alma and waited to see what her surprise was. I was so excited for her. My heart felt like it was beating out of my chest. Alma then pulled out a stack of papers and a set of gold keys. "Wait, my parents bought Alma a new car" I thought.

Alma was unsure what the keys were for so my mother spoke up. "Alma we have put in that envelope your last paycheck with a fifty thousand dollar bonus attached to it. We also have included in that envelope keys to your new home. We know how much you love the ocean, so we purchased you a three-bedroom ocean front beach home. Everything is paid for. The only thing you have to do is sign the documents and move in. Also its only five miles from here so you can visit anytime you want to," my mom said.

What the heck! My parents bought Alma a beach house as a parting gift. I knew they had money and liked Alma, but damn, this even shocked me. I was happy for Alma. If anyone deserved it she did. Alma was so shocked she just stood there with tears running down her face. She then thanked my parents and gave them both a hug. Alma then turned and faced me. It looked like she was on the brink of a breakdown. It was best to get this goodbye over fast. Alma came over to me and gave me a hug, and held me close to her for a long time.

As Alma stood there holding me, I started to have flashbacks of all the good times she and I had together. I thought about my first day of school. I thought about all of the school field trips she accompanied me on. I thought about all of the shopping trips we went on together. I remembered how happy I was as a kid, when she let me swipe my credit card by myself. I was so happy. As I stood there thinking about Alma, I realized that we had a lot of happy times, her and I, coming up. Nevertheless, I was sure going to miss Alma.

Alma slowly pulled away from me, and to even my surprise, I had tears in my eyes. Everyone knew I wasn't the crying type. I didn't think I would react in such an emotional way. The funny thing was, I wasn't at all embarrassed as tear after tear slowly rolled down my cheeks and fell onto my blue blouse. Alma gave me another quick hug and told me to keep in contact with her. She assured me that I could come visit her at her new home anytime I wanted. She took one last look at everyone and she then quietly exited my parents' house. My heart was heavy. I knew she was doing more than exiting my parents' house. She was exiting my life.

The next day I woke up as soon as the sun started peeking through the blinds in my bedroom. Today was going to be epic. I was going to pick up the new car my parents bought me for my eighteenth birthday. They had not told me what kind of car it was, but I did know whatever it was it was going to be expensive. That alone was enough to excite me. I took a quick shower and then put on my pink Chanel jumpsuit, and my pink Gucci pumps to match. I gave my hair a quick brush over and I was ready to go. I couldn't help but wonder what kind of car my parents had bought me. Was it a Range Rover, or a Benz, or Lexus? I didn't have a clue, but I knew I would look classy driving it, whatever it was.

I ran out of my room and downstairs to look for JT. "JT!" I called. I knew he was there. I was ready to go. He was never late for anything. JT came running out of the kitchen "What's wrong Jewel?" he said with panic in his voice. "Nothing, it's time to go pick up my car!" I screamed with excitement. "Let's go!" I yelled. I grabbed JT by the arm and was practically dragging him out the door. He stopped to set the alarm on the house as I stood by the door waiting impatiently. After JT set the house alarm we both headed out the front door. If I had to wait any longer I was going to go crazy. I all but ran out the front door when I froze dead in my tracks.

All I could do was scream. I looked over at JT and he just had a silly smirk on his face. I playfully socked him in the arm. He had known all along. This explained why he wasn't in a rush to leave this morning. There parked in our circular driveway, with a pink bow on top, was a brand new Maserati. Once again I knew my parents had money, but damn, even I didn't expect a Maserati! It was beautiful too. It was the classiest car I had ever seen. It was all cream on the outside and had a cream and pink interior. I ran down off of the porch and started walking around my new car. I couldn't believe it. This was insane.

They even had Aluminum Alloy rims put on my car. I knew they were probably custom made because I had never even seen anything remotely close to the rims I had. I opened the driver's side door and got in the driver's seat. It had that new car smell. Then I screamed in delight again. All of the seats had my name embroidered on them, along with the rugs. I couldn't wait to take my new car downtown. I would definitely turn heads in this car. Everyone would be looking at me, from the young to the old. I knew my parents would buy me something cool and expensive. I was their daughter and they weren't going to have me just driving anything. Their reputation was on the line.

"JT, hop in. We're going for a ride!" I yelled. JT glanced over at me nervously. He knew I could drive, but he also knew I didn't officially have a driver's license yet. I had taken and finished my training, but I was still waiting for my official license to come in the mail. I assured JT that the paper driver's license was just as good as the plastic. JT could be so old-fashioned at times. He finally opened the door and slid in beside me. He looked at me and smiled, and then put on his seat belt. I could tell that even JT was impressed with the car's beauty.

I put on my seat belt and pushed the ignition button to start the car. I was just starting to pull out the driveway when my cell phone rang. I quickly looked at the screen. It was my parents. I put the car back in park and answered the phone. "Hi mom, Thank you and dad so much for the new car! I love it! JT and I were just about to go for a ride downtown in it," I said. My mother replied "You're welcome Jewel; we wanted you to have the best. Listen, your dad and I are coming by tonight to talk to you about something. Expect us around 5:00 p.m.," she said. "Okay mom, I will be there," I replied.

That was strange; I thought my parents were going to be in Paris that week. Whatever they want to talk to me about must be pretty important. I kind of had an idea anyway. My dad had been hounding me lately about what college I was going to attend. Honestly, I had not even thought about it. Why should I go to college anyway? My parents were already rich. I just couldn't see the point. Anyway I wasn't going to let that conversation put a damper on my excitement for my new car. I found my favorite radio station, put on my seat belt, and peeled out of the driveway. I headed uptown to do some shopping. I would deal with my parents and their concerns later.

I picked up a few things at the mall. Then I decided it was time to see what my new car could do on the highway. As I entered the ramp to get on to the highway, I turned up the music, opened my sunroof, and put my stilettos to the metal. I went flying down the highway weaving in and out of traffic. This was a beautiful vehicle. Even though the engine in this car was huge I felt like I was riding on a cloud. I was handling those curves and bends in the road like I had been born to drive this car. It felt awesome. I sat back and let the wind blow through my hair.

After a few seconds, I heard JT clear his throat to get my attention. I looked over at JT and started laughing. I was enjoying myself so much I almost forgot he was with me. The look on his face caused me to laugh hysterically. He looked like he had seen a ghost. He pointed to the odometer and I looked down at it. I had been doing a little bit over one hundred miles per hour. "Holy Cow!" I thought. It didn't even feel like I was driving that fast. I eased my foot up off the pedal and the car started to slow down. The color started to come back into JT's face. No wonder he looked terrified, I thought.

I couldn't help but laugh again. I had damn near given JT a heart attack. I laughed to myself. At least if he did go into cardiac arrest, I could get him to a hospital faster that any ambulance. I was definitely going to have fun with this car. JT and I stopped at the mall to pick up some new things. I had to have a nice expensive new wardrobe to match my new car. It was about 5:15p.m. when JT said, "Jewel we really need to be heading back home. Your parents will be waiting for us. You know your parents' time is very limited."

"Yeah, we better head back," I replied. On the way back home I couldn't help but let my mind wander back to what my parents wanted to talk to me about. I had been sort of hinting to them that, now that I'm 18, I need my own space. I mean, I was technically grown. The previous week I had emailed my mother some information on the lavish new penthouses they were building downtown.

I wanted to rent one of those penthouses. They came already furnished. They had a private entrance. They also had a 24 hour doorman service and access to a full-time housekeeper. That penthouse would be perfect for me. The best thing about it was the fact that it was near all of the hottest shopping centers, and the outlet mall was a half a block away. It was literally within walking distance, but now that I had my new car I was never walking anywhere again. I was going to take my new car everywhere.

I had to keep it clean also. I already knew where I was taking it to be detailed. They had just opened a new detail shop downtown called Twice Az Clean. They only cleaned high-end vehicles. JT sometimes took my parents' limo up there to be cleaned once a week. I had gone up there with him a few times. Let me tell you, some of those cars were filthy, but by the time they left, they looked like they had just come off a showroom floor. They definitely had a talent for bringing new life and class back into those high end-vehicles.

I have to call and talk to the owner because this girl was not waiting for anyone. I wanted them to start on my car as soon as I pulled up. I wanted a standing appointment to have my Maserati cleaned at least once a week. I look good at all times and I wanted my car to look good at all times. By the time JT and I pulled up in front of my house it was 5:45p.m. I spotted my dad's black Bentley parked in the driveway. I prayed we had not kept them waiting too long, or else I was definitely going to hear about it.

I quickly pulled up behind my dad's car and parked. Then JT and I got out and quickly entered the house. He went towards the back to the TV room and I walked around looking for my parents. "Mom, Dad I'm back, where are you?" I yelled. Then I heard my Dad's loud baritone voice echo from the dining room. "We are in here Jewel, come join us," he said. I quickly made my way over to the dining room. They had ordered mom's favorite dish of grilled chicken and sautéed vegetables. The closer I got, the stronger was the aroma of the food.

I spotted the containers on the dining room table. I knew dad had the food delivered from my mother's favorite Mediterranean restaurant uptown. They normally didn't deliver their food but they made sure my mother got some brought to her whenever she was in town. I'm pretty sure they got a hefty tip for the special delivery too. I wasn't hungry when I was out with JT, but since coming into the house and smelling that food all of a sudden felt like I was starving. "Hey mom and dad, I'm sorry we kept you waiting. JT and I took my new car out for a drive. It drives like a dream. I want to thank you again. I love everything about it. It's truly a beautiful car and it suits me perfectly. It has class and cash written all over it," I said.

"Speaking of cash, how much did you guys spend on that car? There was a lot of custom made work on it," I asked. My father spoke up. "That's not important Jewel. We had it custom made to fit your taste and needs. It doesn't matter how much it cost. You know when it comes to money that's not an issue. Let's just say we paid the price of a small mansion uptown. Now take a seat please, we need to talk to you about something more important than money," he said.

I took a seat at the dining room table and thought to myself, nothing is more important than money if you ask me. The maid had already fixed my plate and placed it on the table across from my parents. I poured myself a glass of wine and then started eating. Yes, my parents let me drink wine even though I was underage. It was only when I was around them that I could drink. I wasn't allowed to drink in public until I was 21. My mother tells me underage drinking in public is distasteful, and she didn't want me embarrassing them in any shape or form.

So whenever I was with my parents, which was once in a blue moon, I had a glass of wine, or two. We all sat in silence and ate our food until I looked up at my mom. She had the oddest look on her face. She looked over at my father and he nodded at her and then said, "Jewel there are two weeks left until you graduate. What do you plan on doing about college or a career?" I damn near choked on my grilled chicken. This question totally threw me off. What does she mean a career? Does she mean as in work? I was totally confused. "Well I never really thought about college or working or anything. I never thought I had to. I mean you both are very wealthy, and I have a trust fund, right? Why do I need to go to college? What's the point?" I asked.

I felt like I wasn't college material, and I definitely wasn't working woman material. I was still young and my parents were rich, so what would be the point in me wasting my time going to college? All of these thoughts rapidly ran through my head, as I tried to figure out why my parents were bringing this nonsense to me all of a sudden. Then my dad spoke up, "Jewel you have to realize your mother and I went to one of the top medical schools in the country. We worked hard to amass our wealth. You also have to realize that when you have as much money as we do, people try to take advantage of you all the time. When we are dead and gone, and you inherit our wealth, we need to make sure you are intelligent enough to make smart investments with our money."

"We want this for you so even your children can benefit from our wealth. You don't need to go to medical school like your mother and I. We think it would be wise if you enrolled in the Business Administration Masters program. The dean of The University of California is a member at the country club your mother and I attend. UOC has one of the best business colleges in the country. Your mother and I performed his face-lift a few years ago and he owes us a favor. All we have to do is say the word and you can enroll and start taking classes," he said.

I looked over at my mother and wondered if this was her idea. Then my mom said, "Honey you have to also remember you are a reflection of your father and I. We are well respected in the local community and around the world. We would like to keep it that way. We don't want our friends thinking you are just some out-of-control, uneducated teenager running around town spending our money. We don't want that negative image in their heads. We really just want you to do what's best for everyone," she said.

I sat there with my mouth hanging open. I really didn't know what to say. I put my fork down, and pushed the plate of food slightly away from me. I knew I had just lost my appetite after hearing what I just heard. I couldn't understand why they cared what their colleagues thought of me anyway. I didn't cross paths with any of them on a regular basis. I barely saw them at social functions. They never paid attention to me. Why would it change now that I was grown? "Mom, I don't think it's a good idea at all. I'm mature enough to make good decisions when it comes to money. Why don't you just hire me an accountant or an assistant if you're concerned about how much I'm spending? I don't think the whole college thing is for me," I said. "I'm going to graduate soon and I don't want to jump right back into school," I whined.

My father said, "Jewel, unfortunately you don't have a choice. Your mother and I expect you to be an adult about this and look at it in a positive manner. We would not feel comfortable with you being a beneficiary on our will or having a trust fund, without you having some kind of a business college education." I stared at my mother pleading with my eyes to make her change her mind. I knew she could see that I wasn't happy with what they were doing. If I could change one of their minds I had a chance. My mom stared back at me as if to say "what your father says goes."

I sat there staring at the both of them like they were insane. I couldn't believe they were doing this to me. They were more concerned with how their friends would see me, and their money. They didn't care how I felt. I didn't want to have to go to college, and I was dreading it. The most disappointing thing about the situation was I would end up working anyway if they cut off my trust fund. I was definitely backed into a corner on this one. I didn't have a choice. My parents were practically forcing me to go to college. I knew what I had to do and I was not happy. Pissed off would be the right word to describe it. I knew I had to go to college.

I hated feeling like I was being controlled even as an adult. My parents sat there looking at me as I rolled my eyes and pouted like a two year old. This was unfair and they knew it. Once I had calmed down a little bit I was able to talk. "Well I guess I'm going to college; when do I start?" I said it with just enough attitude to make my mom's eyebrows rise, but not enough for her to say anything. "Jewel, we knew you would make the right decision. We knew you wouldn't let us down. Now we can sleep peaceful at night. As for when you start, we think it would be okay if you enjoyed your summer and started fresh in the fall with everyone else. We assumed correctly that you would make the right decision, so your mother and I took the liberty of buying you a little gift for you to use before you start college. Tell her what it is London," my father urged.

"Well honey you are a grown woman now, and we know you are going to want to be treated like an adult. We need a little more time to think about the penthouse you want to move into. We kind of thought it would be best for you to stay on campus anyway so you get the whole college experience. Your father and I have purchased you a ticket for a seven day cruise to the Bahamas. We have been there several times and we think that would be the perfect place for you to go relax before starting school. The cruise ship is called Paradise, and it is very beautiful and exclusive. We have a friend that owns a beach house in Nassau, and he says you are welcome to stay in it for a week. Just call and let us know when you are ready to leave and we will arrange for a jet to come get you and bring you back to the states when your vacation is over," she said.

"This is the first vacation you will be taking alone as a young woman. We are going to ask JT to sit this one out so you can enjoy yourself. We trust you to go alone. We are going to turn on the GPS on your phone should something happen, and we need to know where you are, but your phone has to remain on for it to work," my mother said.

"A cruise and a vacation by myself!" I screamed. This was going to be epic. I guess they wanted to somewhat show me they were sorry for basically forcing me to go to college. I must admit after hearing that, a vacation did soften the blow a little bit. I was feeling a better.

I smiled and said, "Thanks Mom and Dad." They both said you're welcome at the same time. I asked, "So when do I leave?" "You leave in two weeks Jewel, the day after graduation," my father said. I couldn't believe it. I was going to have so much fun. I could only imagine. I needed a new wardrobe. I needed new swimsuits and beach wear. There was no way I was going to the Bahamas and not look my best. I got up from the dining room table and hugged both of my parents, and then excused myself from the dining room. I went up to my room. I had so much to do and think about.

The next couple of days flew by. I was busy getting all of my transcripts together and filling out my college application. It was a good thing my cap and gown had already been ordered. I had been extremely busy. I did, however, find time in between all the mayhem to go shopping for my vacation. I found some really cute Michael Kors swimsuits and matching sandals at Macy's. I even found time to refresh all of my beach accessories. I purchased so many straw hats and Prada shades it was insane. I was destined to be the classiest lady on the beach. With my new things I didn't think that was going to be a problem.

The rest of that week flew by and before I knew it, it was graduation day. I was so excited about going on my vacation. I couldn't pay any attention to the commencement ceremony. The whole ceremony was a blur to me. I was very happy to see that my parents had invited Alma to my graduation. I could tell she was very proud of me. I had never seen Alma smile so hard. I bet she felt like her own child was graduating. I'm glad I could make her so happy. My parents were smiling, and clapping but they looked awkward sitting in the crowd. They were the only parents overdressed. My mother had on a white cocktail dress, and a white straw hat to match. My father had on an all white three piece suit. My mother wore so many diamonds, the sun kept reflecting off of her jewelry. She was sparkling from every angle. You would have thought they were meeting the queen instead of going to a high school graduation. I had to laugh silently to myself because I knew my parents always went overboard with everything. They had money and they were never afraid to show it.

After the graduation my parents took everyone to dinner. They chose to take us to my favorite Italian restaurant downtown in Brittany Square. This restaurant was always packed, and tonight was no different. My parents knew the owners of the restaurant so we were able to get right in and seated at one of their best tables. The food was fabulous like always, but I didn't have much of an appetite. I did manage to get a few bites of lasagna in though. I didn't want to upset my parents. After we all had dinner and tiramisu for dessert, we decided to leave.

I hugged Alma and thanked her for coming to my graduation. I promised her I would stay in contact, and that I would come visit her as soon as I returned from my vacation. My parents hugged me and said goodbye. They had a car waiting to take them to the airport. They had to speak at a plastic surgeons' convention the next morning, so they were taking a late flight back to Paris. JT didn't go to dinner with us. He was waiting outside in the Limousine to take me home.

Once we made it to the house I decided to go straight to bed. I had packed all of my things the previous day. I knew with everything going on the day of graduation, I wouldn't have time to pack that night. My parents had arranged for JT to drive me to the airport rather early the following morning. They had also arranged for a jet to take me to the port of Miami to board the Paradise cruise ship. It felt so good to lie down in my bed. It had been a long draining day. As soon as my head hit the pillow I went right to sleep.

The next morning the alarm clock went off at 6:00 a.m. I jumped out of bed and immediately started getting ready. This was the day of the trip and I didn't plan on any setbacks. I was ecstatic. I still couldn't believe my parents were letting me take a vacation by myself.

I was definitely starting to feel like a young adult. At 7:15 a.m. I was sitting in the back of my parent's limo on the way to the airport. My heart was beating faster and faster the closer we came to the airport. I was overwhelmed with excitement. Once we arrived JT got my luggage from the trunk, and came around and gave me a hug. "Be careful baby girl. Have fun, and don't forget your parents want you to contact them as soon as you get settled. I will see you when you get back," he said.

I assured JT I would call my parents. I gave him a quick kiss on the cheek, and grabbed my luggage and boarded my parents' jet. I had flown on this jet before, but I had never become accustomed to flying. It still scared the daylights out of me. Thank God the flight was short and sweet. It seemed like we were landing within 30 minutes of the boarding. Once we landed there was a limo waiting to take me to the port of Miami. The ride from the airport to the port was short as well.

I was so excited I started to twirl my hair and tap my feet, which was something I did when I was extremely nervous or excited. The suspense was killing me. We pulled up to the dock and the driver got out and opened the door. I got out of the back seat of the limo and I saw her, the Paradise cruise ship. I'm sure my eyes were as big as two-fifty cent pieces. My mouth just hung open and I was speechless. There the ship stood. It was all white and absolutely beautiful.

I grabbed my luggage and headed over to the window marked "check-in." The older lady at the window informed me that my parents had paid extra money for VIP boarding. This worked out great because I don't do well waiting in lines. The teller also assured me that my room was ready, and I could board whenever I wanted. "Let's go!" I yelled to the limo driver. He grabbed my luggage and I ran towards the cruise ship.

We arrived at the boarding ramp ship and a smiling handsome crew member was waiting to take my VIP boarding pass. He reminded me of the model Tyson Beckford. He had the body of someone who worked out religiously, and soon he began to speak. He had a sexy

English accent. I was beginning to become a bit flushed in the face over this young man. He took my hand, raised it to his mouth and kissed it. He glanced at my ticket and said "Welcome Miss Jewel. Welcome aboard. I will escort you to your room." "Thank you," I replied. I was in love with the ship already. I was ready to relax, party, and relax some more. The handsome crew member escorted me to my room and brought in my luggage. I must say, the room was gorgeous and it had a perfect view of the ocean. I must say they definitely had taste. They knew how to impress their VIP customers. The room looked like a hotel suite. I really loved the whirlpool in the bathroom. The room also had a huge flat screen TV, and a fully stocked mini-fridge. I also had access to my own personal butler. Although the room was nice, I was not trying to be confined in this room no matter how beautiful the view. I wanted to see the ocean first hand.

I locked my room and made my way to the upper deck to take in the view. I found a lounge chair on the deck, reclined back in the chair and took in the view. I could get used to this lifestyle. I could see why my parents worked so hard to achieve this expensive lifestyle. I saw why they liked the finer things in life. The same cute crew member who showed me my room, walked by me with a tray of wine in his hand. I motioned for him to come over and bring me a glass of wine. "Are you 21 Miss Jewel?" he asked. Damn it! I was honestly not expecting him to ask my age but, I knew how to handle the situation. I pulled a fifty dollar bill from my bra and handed it to him and replied, "Of course, I'm twenty 21."

He just looked at me as if he was contemplating taking the bait. I knew he was thinking whether his job was worth serving wine to someone underage. So I made the decision for him. I looked at his name tag and saw his name. "Listen Oliver, you stick around with that tray of yours for the duration of my trip and I will make sure I have my friend Ulysses S. Grant available to you every time. This could turn out to be a very profitable job for you." Oliver smiled and slid the fifty dollar bill in his jacket and handed me a glass of wine. "Enjoy your drink ma'am, "he said.

This cruise was going to be a blast. It just kept getting better and better. I now knew with a little bit of cash I would have these crew members bringing me whatever I wanted. After all, I was a VIP and should be treated like one. I was going to be thousands of miles away from my parents. They wouldn't have a clue what was going on. It just goes to show you that with money you can have anything. A lot of people will sell their souls to the devil for the right price. This vacation was going to be out of this world. I took a sip of wine and laid back and waited for the ship to set sail. However, in all the excitement I had forgotten all about calling my parents.

Jewel Present Time

Boom, Boom, Boom! The crewman banged on Jewel's door and yelled, "Ma'am wake up, wake up!" He didn't get an immediate response so he banged on the door again. This time he heard shuffling feet inside, so he withheld a third knock. He had awoken Jewel from a very peaceful, alcohol-induced sleep. Once she heard the banging she quickly jumped out of bed. She looked over at the bedside clock and wondered who the heck would be knocking on the door this late into the night. She stumbled her way across the living room towards the door, almost tripping over her high heels along the way. "I need to take it easy on the wine," she thought.

Jewel yanked the door open and yelled, "What do you want you idiot? Do you know what time it is? Is this the kind of treatment you give to your first class customers?" She stared at the crew member standing outside her door and he looked terrified. "I'm sorry ma'am, but something terrible has happened. I need you to quickly put some clothes on and follow me to the upper deck immediately. There has been a terrible accident with the ship and the captain has issued an emergency evacuation," he said. I looked at him like he had to be out of his freaking mind.

Was I hearing this correctly? Evacuate the ship? What the hell was going on? I looked the crew man in his eyes and said," You have 5 seconds to tell me what the hell is going on here. Is this some sort of sick joke? If I have been woken up out of my sleep for a joke, someone is going to lose their damn job come sunrise. Now you better get to explaining!" I stood there looking at the crew member trying to detect a sign of foolishness, but there wasn't any. In fact, he still had the same terrified look on his face that he had when he arrived.

I figured this just may be the real deal. "Okay let me get my things together, and then I will be up," I said. I then closed the door leaving the crew member standing there. I turned around to start gathering my clothes and other personal items to put in my suitcase. I heard someone banging on my door again. Boom, boom, boom! "Oh what now?" I thought. I went over to the door and once again yanked it open. The same crew member was standing there. "Ma'am you don't understand, this ship is sinking. You don't have time to pack your belongings. You need to come with me now!" He made sure he yelled the word "now" rather loudly to get his point across.

He then grabbed my arms and pulled me out of the door. He practically dragged me down the hall and up the stairs. I started yelling and screaming curse words at him. I told him my parents were going to sue the shit out of this boat. Once we got to the upper deck, I was able to look around and analyze everything that was going on. I went mute. There were hundreds of people being lead over to the ship's life boats. Some were screaming and many were crying. There were men and women trying to get back down to their rooms to grab personal items, but the crew members were stopping them and bringing them back.

I felt their pain. I had left at least $50,000 worth of things in my room. I couldn't believe what I was seeing. These people had been dragged out of their rooms and brought up there also. A lot of them still had on their night clothes. I was grateful I had come back to my room and passed out in my Louis Vuitton jumpsuit because I was still wearing it. I reached down and felt my pants pocket; I still had my cell phone. "Thank God," I thought. As soon as I got into one of those life boats, I was going to call for my own help.

They started loading up the lifeboats with the women first. I noticed they were only putting a small number of women in the lifeboats when they could have easily fit many more. I was instructed to get into a lifeboat with three other women. They all looked as confused and scared as everyone else. Before I could find a spot to sit they started lowering us down the side of the ship. Once the life boat was lowered to within five feet of the ocean they pulled the ropes and let it fall into the ocean. The ropes were quickly yanked back up to let down the next one.

I don't know why, but once the life boat hit the water and we were sitting out there alone, the realization of what was going on started to hit me like a ton of bricks. I thought to myself that the situation was absolutely crazy. I was just starting to have the time of my life on this trip. I couldn't believe these people. Wait until my parents found out about their negligence. I had to leave all of my new things behind. Somebody was going to be reimbursing me for everything I lost on this damn cruise. By the time my parents get through suing the owners of the ship, it would never set sail again.

The life boat started to drift further and further away from the ship and the other lifeboats. How in the world where they going to rescue us if we were spread out all over the Atlantic Ocean? I looked around at the other women on the boat. None of them had said a word. Two of them looked to be my age. One was looking off into space and the other was crying. The one who was looking off into space looked like a homeless teenager. She looked a mess. Her clothes were old and ragged. She was most likely a stowaway who had snuck on the ship. Then there was a middle-aged lady who had her hands in the praying position. I didn't know about them, but I was not going to stand for being stranded out there on the ocean.

I reach down and grabbed my cell phone out of my pocket. I would call for my own help. I wasn't going to sit around and wait. I tried my parents' number first. The phone beeped two times and then dropped the call. "What the hell," I yelled. I tried their number again and the same thing happened. I looked down at the screen and it indicated "no signal". I disconnected the call and put the phone back into my pocket. "Just fucking great! I spend $1,000 dollars on one of the most advanced cell phones out on the market and I can't even get a damn signal over the Atlantic Ocean!" I yelled.

I had to sit there and wait like the rest of the commoners. I knew that if my parents had not heard from me by sun-up they would know something was wrong. They would try to call me and wouldn't get an answer. Then they would turn on the GPS tracking on my phone and locate me. They would send the Coast Guard out to look for me. My parents had money and loads of it, and would do whatever it took to find me.

I sat back in the lifeboat and looked up at the stars. I still couldn't believe that what was going on was real. I especially couldn't believe it was happening to me. I had planned on having a great vacation. I viewed the vacation as being an initiation into adulthood. Instead, I get on a cruise ship with a crew that manages to sink it. My vacation was a nightmare. I would not be going on any more cruises after this. My parents were just going to have to buy me a yacht. At least I knew nothing this crazy would happen on my own boat.

I hoped that Oliver was okay. I looked over at the other women on the boat. We couldn't do anything except wait for help. I knew they were scared, and honestly, deep down, I was scared too. I didn't want to think about what could happen to us out there. I knew somebody had to be looking for us. I didn't want to die, my young life was just beginning. I still had all of that money waiting for me in my trust fund when I turned 21. I couldn't die before my parents, that's not how it's supposed to work. I knew by early morning my parents would have someone looking for me. I just had to be patient. If I could just make it a few hours out there on the ocean I would be okay.

GISELLE'S STORY

"And that's a wrap Giselle. I think we have another great track on our hands. You are killing the music game right now," Chris said. Chris was my producer. We had just completed the first single for my second album. I took my headphones off and stepped outside of the recording booth. I must admit, even I was exhausted. I was glad we had finally finished the song. Chris and I and the rest of my production crew had been in the studio for eight hours working on the single. Everyone knew Chris was a perfectionist. We knew what we were headed for when we went into the studio. We weren't leaving until we had perfected every beat, every lyric, and gotten Chris's stamp of approval.

It was going to be a long night. I never challenged any of Chris's decisions when it came to music. The man was a lyrical genius. I had a beautiful singing voice, but he was the reason behind a good portion of my success. He wrote a lot of my material, and had personally picked out many of my beats and melodies. I currently had one album out that Chris produced and it had gone double platinum. We were beginning to work on my second album. I was praying it would have just as much success as the first one. I had a good feeling it would because I was working with one of the best producers in the industry. Chris was also very knowledgeable about other aspects of the music industry. He booked all of my performances and interviews. I'm so glad we found each other. Before meeting Chris I was ready to give up on music and didn't think I would ever land a recording contract.

I started packing up my things I had brought to the studio. I took a minute to reflect on my life. I looked around the studio and I couldn't do anything but smile. It had been a long tough road for me. I had finally started to live what I had always dreamed, though some of the situations and losses I had endured had scarred me forever. It wasn't always peaches and cream for me. Just one year ago I was ready to give up on music, and the prospect of ever having a recording contract. Just two years ago I had lost my mother to cancer.

Losing my mother was one of the hardest losses I ever suffered. She had always been my rock. Even though it had been two years, those wounds were still very fresh. If I close my eyes I can still see her face. My mother was beautiful. I had never met a woman more stunning than her. She had the smoothest caramel colored skin I had ever seen. She didn't have a pimple or a blemish anywhere. She had natural beauty. She never wore an ounce of makeup, and if you had the privilege of meeting her you would know why. It would have been insulting to cover up my mother's natural beauty.

She had big beautiful brown eyes. I have those same big brown eyes. They are identical to my mother's. I use to think my mom could see into a person's soul with her eyes. My grandma use to tell me my mother could hypnotize people with her eyes, and if you stared at her for more than a few seconds you were in trouble. You were then her puppet whether you realized it or not. My mother had exceptional features. She had a perfect nose and lips. A lot of women would ask her what physician did her nose job. She would just laugh and answer back, "God created me baby. I haven't had any surgeries." I guess they felt it was rare for an African American woman to have the features my mother had.

My mother never wore lipstick, but her lips were naturally a shade of pink. So she looked like she wore lipstick all of the time. I always prayed as a little girl that I would grow up to look like my mother. My grandma always says my mother favored model Beverly Johnson in the 70's when she was at the start of her career. Grandmother was Cherokee Indian, and her family was all of the same tribe. She had long, thick black hair. She was almost seventy so she had pretty strands of grey throughout. My mother had inherited my grandmother's beautiful hair. My mother's hair was long and thick just like my grandmother's. I remember as a little girl my mother always wore her hair up in a huge bun on the top of her head. I always thought she looked like a queen.

The only time she wore her hair down was for special occasions, and when she did everyone was instantly awestruck by her beauty. She was my momma and I saw her every day, but she still even took my breath away at times. As I got older my family would tell me, "Giselle, you look just like your mother," This always put a smile on my face because I knew she was a beautiful lady.

My mother always told me that I would be special in my own unique way. I think this was confirmed to her the day she discovered that I could sing. I was in her room playing dress up one evening. I had picked out her gold and black Tom Ford evening gown and put it on. I had also picked out a pair of her gold Pura Lopez high heeled shoes and slid those on. I had opened her jewelry box and picked out a rather heavy gold chain and bangles to match. Once I felt like the outfit was complete, I went over to her huge dressing mirror and started singing. I had brought my toy microphone I had gotten for my birthday a few months ago.

I started belting out my favorite Whitney Houston song entitled "I Will Always Love You." I had heard my mother playing it numerous times in the car so I knew all of the words. I sang that song like I had written it myself. I was so into singing it that I hadn't noticed my mother walk into the room. I wasn't aware that she had actually been standing there for quite some time. When I spun around in front of the dressing mirror mid song, I noticed that she had been watching me. I stopped singing immediately and froze. She stood there looking at me for the longest time. She didn't look upset, she just stood there looking at me as if she had just witnessed something spectacular.

I know now that the something spectacular was me. I, on the other hand, thought I was going to be in trouble for getting into my mother's things. I slowly started to take off her jewelry as carefully as I could. Then she stopped me, "No, no, baby, you can leave it on." I was confused at first, then when I saw my mother smile at me, I knew I had heard right. I broke into the biggest grin. I put the huge hole in my mouth from a missing tooth on full display. I quickly put the jewelry back on and took my place back in front of the mirror.

Then my mother looked at me and said, "Giselle honey, I didn't know you could sing so beautifully. If I put some more of Whitney's music on can you sing it for me?" I replied, "Oh sure mother, I know most of the words to all of those albums you listen to when you're cleaning the house." My mother went to get more albums to play and I twirled in front of her mirror and waited for her to come back. This was exciting. I had never had an audience when I sang those songs, but I was happy I could sing for my mother.

She and I sat in her room for at least an hour that day. She would play song after song. When I sang a few songs off one album she put on another. I was having a good time. I was excited to be able to put on a show for my mom. I belted those songs out with all my might. I wanted my mother to be proud of me for putting on such a good performance. Some of the songs she played were fast and some were slow. Some of them had low notes and some had really high notes. I sung those songs too even though some of them made me feel like I was screaming the words out.

I sang my little heart out for my mother. When she turned the last song off she clapped really loudly for me and gave me a standing ovation. "Okay baby, that's enough for today," she said. She grabbed me and gave me a huge hug and kiss. "Listen Giselle, I knew you would be special and unique since the day you were born. I knew you were a blessing from God. Giselle, God has blessed you with a gift. That gift is your beautiful voice. Those records I played for you to sing are by women named Patty Labelle, Whitney Houston, and Aretha Franklin. Those ladies are some of the greatest vocalist to grace this earth. Those songs are some of the hardest songs for talented adult women to sing," she went on to say.

"Many women have tried to perform those songs and have failed to pull them off. You just belted out all of those songs like you were in the studio when they recorded them. Very few people have talent like your's Giselle. God has blessed you with this talent, and you should share it with the world," she said. From that day forward my life changed. My mom was determined more than ever to take my music career to the top. I was going to be a singer, and she told me as long as she was living she was going to see it through.

I was just as determined and excited as she was. I loved to sing, and I thought after singing for my mother I would be comfortable singing for others. I didn't feel shy or scared at all. It was like I thrived off having someone watch me perform. I felt that if I had an audience watching I would push myself to do my absolute best. A few days after I performed for my mother she had me performing all over town. I had singing gigs at weddings, festivals, and department store grand openings. I was singing everywhere. My mother entered me in every darn talent show within two hundred miles of our town.

She was determined to see me succeed. She made sure I not only sounded good, but I looked good also. She fixed my hair so pretty, and used a hot comb on my head every Sunday night. I'm telling you, she had a magic touch with that comb because my hair would stay straight and shiny all week. Then we went shopping for new beautiful dresses. They were not like my normal church dresses. These dresses looked like ball gowns, and many of them had rhinestones on them. She always made me perform in a dress. She would tell me, "Giselle, first impressions are very important. A person will see how you present yourself first, and then they will hear your beautiful voice after." She made sure I practiced singing and performing every night after I finished my homework. I went over those songs over and over again. My mother pushed me to be better and better. I didn't mind though because I knew she was my biggest supporter.

Every single talent show my mother entered me into I won with ease. I went up against other children and even other adults and still walked away with the first place trophy. By the time I got to high school, the whole wall in the living room was covered in ribbons and trophies. I sometimes even won cash prizes at the talent shows, so my mom and I decided it was time for me to open a savings account. After I won several talents shows, I had saved up quite a bit of prize money. After 9 years went by I was surprised that I still hadn't signed with any recording labels.

I was doing everything I could to gain more fans, and to bring more exposure to my talents. I had recently started singing at one of the local taverns called Mario's on Friday night. It was just a quick ten minute set but I was excited nonetheless. I was always wishing a big city record producer would hear me sing one night and offer me a record deal. I wasn't being paid to sing at Mario's, but I wanted the exposure. By the time I started my senior year in high school every-one in town knew who I was and what I had to offer. Many people told me I was the next generation's Whitney Houston.

It seemed like the older I got the more determined my mother was to make me a star. Even though I was still looking for my big break, she never gave up on me. She never lost faith in me. If I got discouraged she made sure to tell me," Your time is coming Giselle, I can feel it." I tried my best to stay positive and optimistic, but I had been doing talent shows and singing at events since I was a little girl. It was hard not to get discouraged. The older I got, the more worried I became about my future. My mother and I had spent so many years perfecting my talent, we never gave thought what might happen if I didn't get a recording contract.

By the time I graduated high school, I was starting to rethink the whole idea of becoming a singer. The older I got the more responsi-bilities I accrued. I was paid for singing at the weddings and sporting events, but it wasn't enough to make a living. While having a par-ticularly bad day I expressed this concern to my mother. She, to my surprise, went ballistic. She did something that day that I had never experienced, and that's raise her voice at me.

She said, "Listen Giselle, I don't want to hear that kind of negativity come out of your mouth again! I didn't raise you to be a quitter! Your time is coming; you have to have faith that it's going to happen. I have never stopped believing in you, and I never will. I know your potential and the rest of the world will soon enough." I stood in front of her looking her intently in the face. Then I started to cry. She was absolutely right; I had come too far to give up now. I had to listen to my mother's advice and have faith that my time to shine would come.

My mother came over to me and wrapped me in her arms. I laid my head on her shoulder and she just held me for a few seconds. I instantly started felling better just being in my mother's embrace. She gave me a tight squeeze and then slowly lifted my chin up until we were face to face and said, "Giselle, I want you to promise me that no matter what happens you will keep singing. I may not be here years from now to enjoy your success, but my spirit will always be with you. You have to promise me that you will never stop trying."

I stood and wiped the tears from my eyes. "I promise momma, I won't let you down," I said. I reached over and gave my mother another hug and, without words, we both knew that I was okay. I had gained my confidence. I was always grateful for her positive words. She always knew how to get me back on track. I really was very fortunate to have such a supporting and loving mother in my life. My father had left her when I was just a small child, but she worked hard and made sure I always had what I needed, and that I had a safe place to call home. I was praying that one day I could be half the woman my mother was. I left her in the kitchen and went upstairs to work on new material. That talk with her gave me a fresh new outlook on my music career.

That next week I went back to singing at weddings festivals and other big events. I started traveling even further to enter talent shows, even across state lines. I wanted my voice and my music to reach as many people as possible. I was still winning all of the talent shows that I entered. I felt like I was finally reaching out to more people and letting my voice be heard in many places. I was getting tons of exposure. I was praying the right person would approach me and my music career would take off. I was more determined now than I had ever been. I was working on my lyrics and taking voice lessons all the time. I felt that I had reached the prime of my potential.

I was feeling positive until something terrible happened. My mother told me that she had epithelial cancer. I would later find out she had been diagnosed many years before. She had made the decision to not tell me as a young girl. I still remember that dreadful, yet beautiful day. I had just finished singing at a friend's wedding. It took place in a back yard and the weather was perfect. I had originally taken a taxi to the wedding, but after the wedding reception the weather was so nice I decided to walk the four short blocks home. It felt so good to be outside in the fresh air. The temperature was in the low 70's with a mild breeze.

I started out walking and enjoying that beautiful evening, then two blocks in I started to jog. I'm pretty sure I was getting some strange looks from the people I jogged past. I was, after all, wearing a formal dress and flat ballet shoes. It felt good to have the wind in my face. I could see the look of confusion on some of the passersby's faces. They weren't sure if I was jogging or running from someone. I'm pretty sure the dress is what threw them off. I didn't mind, it felt good to get my blood pumping.

As I continued jogging I looked around and noticed the nice small town we lived in. Some of the families on our block had been living there since I was a little girl. Suddenly my cell phone started ringing, breaking my train of thought. I looked at the screen and saw that it was my mother calling. I quickly stopped running and answered my phone, "Hey mom," I said, slightly out of breath. "Hey Honey," she responded. "Listen I need you to come home. I have something to talk to you about. It's very important," she said. "Mom what's wrong?" I asked with just a hint of panicked shakiness in my voice. "Giselle, just please come home right away. I will talk to you when you get here," she said. "Okay mom, I'm one block away I will be there shortly," I told her.

I ended the call and started running home. Now I was running down the block at full speed, like my life depended on it. I was running so fast you would have thought I was Gail Devers in the 1992 Barcelona Olympics. All I kept thinking about as I ran was what my mother had to talk to me about. The closer I got to the house the more nervous I became. She didn't sound like her usual cheerful self. She sounded sad and that worried me.

I made it home in record time. I ran up the front steps and threw open the front door. I looked around downstairs yelling "Mom, MOM, Where are you?" Then I heard her answer from upstairs; "I'm in your room Giselle, come on up." I quickly took the stairs two at a time and ran down the hallway to my room. My mother was sitting on my bed with her legs crossed in front of her. "Hey baby," she said. "Grab your brush off of your vanity and come over here and brush momma's hair for her." After my mother said that my jaw hit the floor. I hadn't brushed her hair since I was a little girl. It was my favorite thing to do as a child.

I used to love the feel of running the brush through her long thick hair. She would even sometimes let me braid it all up into a long French braid down her back. As I got older that was one of the happiest memories I had of my mother and I. Now after so many years had gone by she was asking me to do it again. I eagerly grabbed the brush off my vanity and went over and started brushing her hair. I instantly felt like a little girl again. I stood behind her brushing her hair and, for a few minutes, no words were spoken.

Then my mother spoke up; "Giselle, I have something to tell you. It breaks my heart for me to have to tell you this. When you were just a young girl, I was diagnosed with epithelial ovarian cancer. It's the most dangerous of all ovarian cancers. My physician wanted to give me full hysterectomy years ago, but at that particular time in my life I opted not to have the surgery. I was young and you were the only child I had at the time. After discussing treatment with my physicians we decided on chemotherapy to rid my body of the cancer. I later went through a debunking surgery of the ovaries to also remove any remaining cancer cells left behind."

"My doctor informed me at the time that even with these two procedures my chances of surviving greater than six years were only fifty percent. I would be in remission, but no one knew for how long. Presently, there is no cure for epithelial ovarian cancer. After everything I went through, and with my doctors basically handing me down a death sentence, I became extremely depressed. I felt numb and hopeless inside. I didn't want to live my last days wondering when and where the cancer would return. I thought a great deal about how much time I would have when it did return."

"I hid my prognosis and my depression from the world. You were such a small innocent child. I didn't want to turn your innocent world into a nightmare. You may not remember, but a few months after my chemotherapy and surgery, I left you in the care of my mother. I checked myself into a clinic for depression. Those three months changed my life drastically. I came out of that clinic stronger than ever. I came home with a new outlook on life and a new level of self worth. Your father left us when you were an infant. I'd be damned if you were going to lose your mother too."

"I started living my life one day at a time. I started to really appreciate everyday God gave me. I continued to raise you on my own, and as you got older I made the decision to not reveal my diagnosis to you. I wanted you to have a happy childhood. I didn't want you to be burdened by my diagnosis or my past struggles with depression. Giselle, my chances of living past six years were very slim. It has now been 13 years. I have been in remission up until last week. Last week I started having some weird symptoms I wasn't familiar with. All of a sudden I didn't have much of an appetite, and my abdomen became swollen."

"My symptoms were so subtle and vague. I didn't think it was anything serious. I decided to call my doctor anyway. My doctor seemed concerned right away since he knew of my past health issues. He urged me to come in immediately and have a CT scan done. The results came back a few hours later and my worst fears came true. The cancer had come back with a vengeance. It started in my abdomen and spread to other organs. My doctor informed me that the cancer is at stage four. He does not give me more than thirty days to live Giselle," she said.

I sat across from my mother staring at her. I didn't know what to say. I didn't know what to think. My mother was dying, how was I supposed to process this type of information? I felt like what she was saying wasn't true. I saw her everyday and she looked fine to me. She didn't look sick. She couldn't leave me at this time in my life. I needed her so much. She was my biggest supporter. I started singing because of her. I didn't know how I would go on without her. She was my backbone. She kept me going when I was ready to give up, and now she was dying.

All of these thoughts were running through my mind when I dropped the brush I was using on my mother's hair. When I picked it up off the floor there were clumps of my mother's beautiful black hair tangled in it. I held the strands of hair to my cheek and felt its softness. Looking at the amount of her hair in my hands made me realize the truth of what she was telling me. This was not a bad dream I had yet to awaken from. My mother was terminally ill. Suddenly it was all too real. My mother was dying and there was nothing I could do to stop it. At that moment I became angry. All I could think of was why this was happening to us. I threw the brush at the wall and collapsed to the ground. I cried for my mother. I cried for me. I cried for the grandkids that she would never meet.

I couldn't begin to imagine what my life would be like without her. This wasn't supposed to happen to my mother, she was such a kind-hearted person. She didn't deserve to suffer. I thought of all these things as I laid face-down on the floor. The tears kept flowing. I had never cried so hard in my life. I realized at that moment that there really was such a thing as a broken heart. I physically felt like my heart was hurting. I wished it would have been me instead of her. I wished I could trade my life for hers.

My mother came over to me and gently sat me up in front of her. She kissed my forehead, and tried to wipe away the tears that fell uncontrollably from my eyes. "It's okay Giselle; you are going to be okay. My days were numbered years ago, but by the grace of God I was able to see you blossom into a beautiful, strong young lady. I will always be with you, even when I'm dead and gone. My spirit will always be with you. I don't want you to fall into a deep depression like I once did. Let's enjoy the time that we have left together. When my time comes and the good Lord calls me home, you will have beautiful, happy memories of us together," she said.

"Momma, I can't!" I yelled. "I will die without you," I sobbed. "No you won't Giselle, you are stronger than that. I didn't raise you to be weak. Please remember your promise that you made to me about your music. Don't ever stop trying. Don't ever stop singing," she said. "I promise momma. I promise I won't give up" I replied. I laid my head on her shoulder and cried as she rocked me back and forth in her arms. We sat in that room and held each other until the sun came up. I had cried most of the night, and I couldn't cry another tear. I was literally all cried out.

My mother's health began to deteriorate rather rapidly. The cancer had started to destroy other organs in her body at an alarming rate. Two weeks after she told me of her illness she was bedridden and receiving hospice care. The cancer was killing her, and all of her organs were failing. She was beginning to physically look very sickly. She started to lose weight very quickly, because she was unable to eat. Her skin started to become pale and dry. This caused her skin to shed flakes. Her hair had started to become thin and was falling out in chunks. Her eyes are what bothered me the most. They had begun to sink in and the scleras of her eyes were a pale yellow. It broke my heart to see the gruesome effects this sickness was having on my mother. All we could do was give her pain medication to keep her comfortable. I was by her side every chance I could get. It tore me up inside to see her in this state. I didn't want her to suffer, but I didn't want her to die. I felt selfish for not wanting her to leave me, but I

CHANTELLE MALONE

knew that she had endured a great deal of pain. I wished every day I could've of traded places with her.

One evening my mother called me to her bedside. She struggled to sit up and talk to me. She was getting weaker and her breathing was labored. "Momma, lay back down please. You don't have to sit up to talk to me. You are weak," I said. "I'm okay Giselle, I feel okay today. Can you prop me up with a few of those pillows? I want you to brush my hair. It's all tangled from lying down," she said. I knew my mother should be lying down and resting but at this point I didn't want to do anything to upset her so I propped her up. I didn't have the heart to tell her no. I grabbed the brush off the dresser and started brushing her hair. She didn't have much of it left at this stage of her terminal illness.

She looked straight ahead while I brushed her hair. She had a smile on her face. It had been weeks since I had seen her smile. It made me feel good to see it. She looked up at me and I stopped brushing her hair. "Giselle I love you. I want you to always remember that," she said. "I love you too momma," I responded. I brushed her hair a few more minutes and then I started to notice discomfort on her face. "Okay momma, I'm going to lie you back down so you can rest. I know you are uncomfortable. I can see the discomfort on your face," I said.

I put the brush away and helped the nurse lay my mother back in bed. I pulled the cover up to her chin and kissed her cheek. I assured the hospice nurse that I was going to be with momma all night and that she could go home, and come back in the morning. I went downstairs and cleaned up a little, locked the house up and went back upstairs. I had not been sleeping well at all lately. I was exhausted and emotionally drained. I went back up to my mother's room. She had fallen asleep. I whispered in her ear, "I love you" and then curled up in the recliner next to her bed. In a few minutes I was sound asleep.

That night I dreamed of my mother. I saw her in my dreams the way I remember her before she became ill. She was young, beautiful and healthy in my dreams. I dreamed of all the good times

I had shared with her. It was like a slideshow of my life with her, ranging from my young childhood to adulthood. I slept well that night. It was some of the best sleep I had in a long time. The next morning I woke up rather early, and felt good and well rested. I decided to let my mother sleep a little longer before I woke her up for breakfast.

I went downstairs and made a cup of coffee. I thought to myself that maybe I should have my mother's beautician come over to wash and braid her hair so it doesn't get too tangled. I wanted to make sure she felt as comfortable as possible. Sadly, I didn't know at the time that the next time anyone would style my mother's hair would be at her funeral. That morning when I went to wake her up for breakfast, she was not breathing. She had passed away peacefully in her sleep, with me sleeping next to her.

After my mother passed away, I felt like my world had been turned upside down. I was only twenty years old and had lost both of my parents. My mother was gone and I had no clue where my father was. He might as well have been dead too. I went into a deep mourning after my mother passed away. After her funeral I pretty much shut myself off from the world. I stayed in the house in my pajamas. I didn't go anywhere and I didn't take any calls from anyone. After a few weeks went by I started to feel guilty. I promised my mother I wouldn't live that kind of life. I knew she wouldn't approve of me being depressed so I slowly started putting my life back together. I had to keep my promise and not give up on my singing career.

The next week I started entering talent shows, and auditioning for singing roles at the local theatres. I felt like I had to explore every avenue that could potentially lead me to success.

I started singing again at Mario's bar, and performed at a few clubs. I even performed at events out of state. I was doing everything I could to reach as many people as possible. I wanted my voice to be heard. Someone would eventually have to give me a break. If I could just get in a studio and record a few songs, my chances of finding a producer would increase. I knew when they heard my voice on those tracks they would be begging me to sign a contract. The problem was I couldn't afford to buy time in a studio on my own.

Then one night my luck changed. I was singing at a bar called Invy. I had finished my set and was sitting at the bar when a man walked over to me and asked, "What label are you signed to?" My back had been to him, so I spun around on the barstool to see who was talking to me. There in front of me stood a skinny, dark-skinned man in glasses. He was quite a looker. He had a Steve Harvey fade, and beautiful hazel eyes. He was dressed rather odd to just be hanging out in a local bar. I hate to judge people, but to me he looked like a pimp. He had on a three piece striped blue and white suit with the hat to match, and shoes that looked like they were made from some kind of animal skin. He also had on a ton of gold jewelry. I noticed he had a ring on every finger except for the left ring finger. I thought to myself, "Who the heck is this man?"

"Excuse me, do I know you?" I asked. "No, you don't know me yet. My name is Eazy. I just watched you finish your set up there, and I just want to say you got some serious skills. You just sang that Gladys Knight song better than she ever did. You have some real, genuinely raw talent. I was interested in what record label you are signed with," he said. "Well thank you sir, but I'm not signed with a record label right now. I'm in the process of looking for a record producer to help me get signed to a label," I answered back. "You're not signed with anyone? All that talent you have and you're not under a label? You have to be looking in the wrong place because anybody in their right mind would be begging you to sign with their label," he said. "Thank you," I replied..

"Well guess what?" he asked. "What?" I asked with a hint of skepticism in my voice. "Today is your lucky day. I happen to be a music producer and I have my own record label out in California. I'm in town on business. I was on my way back to my hotel when I decided to stop in here for a drink to wind down. You have an amazing voice. I would love to put you in the studio and see what we can come up with. I'm co-owner of a record label, but when my partner hears your voice I'm sure he will be just as convinced as I am. I'm sure he won't hesitate to sign you to the label," Eazy said. "What?" I screamed, "Are you serious? You are a real music producer?" I asked. "Yes I am little lady, in the flesh." "Do you know how long I have been trying to get my singing career off the ground? I have been trying for years," I said. "Well, beautiful, your wait is over. I work with some of the hottest singers in the industry right now, and some of their albums have gone platinum. Your dreams are going to finally come true. Here is a group I am currently working with. You may have heard of them." He pulled a CD from his pocket and handed it to me. I was in total disbelief. It was the CD of a new girl group that was currently burning up the charts.

The group's songs were on the radio constantly. There was word that their CD was headed towards platinum status. "You produced these girls? Get out of here, this is the hottest group out right now!" I yelled. "Read the back of the cover," Eazy urged. I flipped over the CD case and glanced at the list of songs. I noticed that several of the songs had Eazy's name listed as the primary producer. I was in shock. I couldn't believe who was standing in front of me. This could be my big break. I finally had a great shot at getting a record deal. I could finally begin to make dreams become a reality.

Then for some reason I began to feel slightly apprehensive about Eazy's real identity. I scanned Eazy over from head to toe. I thought to myself "Giselle, don't be stupid. I don't even know this man. You just met him in a local bar." I couldn't expect a miracle from someone like that now, could I? I scanned him over once again. Everything that Eazy had on looked very expensive, so I figured he was wealthy. He didn't look to be too much older than me, and too young to be a pimp. I had to take his word for it that he was the producer he identified on the CD. I mean, after all, his name was on the CD.

"What did you say your name was pretty lady?" Eazy asked. "My name is Giselle" I replied. "Giselle, I know how this may look to you, but let me assure you that I am who I say I am. I know you may still feel a little unsure so I'm going to give you a little friendly ultimatum.

I'm going to be in town for another week finalizing a business deal. We can meet up during the week for dinner and get to know each other better. If you feel like you can trust my word by the end of the week, I will fly you out to California and pay for you to record a demo in my studio. If you feel like you can't trust me by the end of the week, then you can stay here, and wonder for the rest of your life if you just passed up the chance of a lifetime. Do we have a deal?" Eazy asked.

For a few seconds I didn't say anything. I was really confused about what I should do. Picking up and moving to California was a huge step. I had never been that far away from my little town before. I had always dreamed of going to California, and knew I had a chance to go and potentially fulfill my dreams of being a singer. This all sounded just too good to be true, but what did I have to lose? I felt like I was out here in the world alone anyway. My mother was the most important person to me, and I had lost her to cancer. I didn't have her there to guide me. It was the first big decision I had to make without her guidance. I knew I had to at least give this young man a chance. It wouldn't be right for me to stereotype him and assume he wasn't being honest. "Okay Eazy: you have a deal. I will have a decision for you by Friday."

"Great, let's meet up tomorrow and you can start to get to know me, and I can get to know my new future platinum artist," he said with a huge grin on his face. I must admit he was rather handsome when he smiled. Eazy and I exchanged numbers and I promised him I would meet up with him the next day. I went home from the bar that evening with a new bounce in my step. I couldn't believe my prayers were being answered. I just wished my mother could have been there to see it.

The next day I met up with Eazy for dinner. He was surprisingly easy to talk to. He was actually pleasant company. He asked me all sorts of questions about myself, from if I had any siblings, to how long I had been singing. I answered all of his questions with ease, until he asked me what my parents and family would think about me going out to California. The look on my face must have given him a clue that he was venturing into a topic I didn't feel comfortable talking about. I didn't want to talk about my mother to Eazy. The grieving for my mother was still very fresh. "Both of my parents passed away when I was younger," I told Eazy. "I'm sorry to hear that Giselle," he said. "Thanks," I responded rather uncomfortably.

Eazy and I both ate our meals in silence for the next couple of minutes. I was grateful that he didn't continue to probe me for details on my parents' death. I decided to lighten up the mood a little bit so I started asking Eazy some questions of my own. I found out he was 31 years old. He had one sister and no brothers, and his parents lived out in California with him. He seemed like he grew up a hard worker like me. He graduated from college with a degree in music production. He went on to tell me that even after college he had a hard time breaking into the music industry. He also told me that this didn't bother him too much because by the time he broke into the business he was more knowledgeable about what it took to be successful.

It began to get late. Eazy paid for our meal and we both promised to meet up the next day. I arrived home that night and sat down at my desk and turned my laptop on. I needed to do a little detective research on Mr. Eazy. I googled Eazy's name and I quickly found several pictures and articles about him. There were articles about recording artists he worked with over the years. There was a huge article in the New York Times Magazine of him accepting a Grammy with an R&B group he was currently producing. It seems he was telling the truth about the group. The article mentioned him as the group's producer, and even gave him credit for producing most of their hit songs.

Next, I searched Eazy's record label that he co-owned. The label was called BeEazy Records. Eazy and a guy named Benjamin Travers owned the company. They had been in business for five years. It seemed like the only articles I found about the record label were fairly positive. I was starting to feel better about dealing with him. I couldn't find anything incriminating, or anything that would lead me to believe that Eazy wasn't the real deal. I shut my computer down and started getting ready for bed. I could only hope that I could get some sleep because I had so much on my mind. I had a lot to think about before Friday.

On Wednesday morning my cell phone woke me up out of my sleep. I looked down at my cell phone and it was Eazy calling me. I wondered what he could want so early in the morning, it was only 6:00 a.m. I let out a small grunt and answered my phone, "Good morning Eazy, what's going on?" I asked. "Good morning beautiful. I need you to get dressed and meet me at the café on Lenox Ave. If possible, I need you to be there by no later than 7:25 a.m.," he said. "Wait, what? I just woke up Eazy. I can't get dressed and be over there in an hour. Why so early anyway?" I whined. "Giselle just trust me, you won't regret it. Now hurry and get dressed so you can make it on time," he urged. "Okay," I said hanging up the phone.

I quickly got out of bed, took a quick shower and found some clothes to put on. I didn't have the energy to dress myself up this early in the morning, so I did my best to look somewhat decent. I quickly put on a pair of jeans, and an Old Navy t-shirt. I kept wondering why in the world Eazy would want to meet up so early in the morning and why it was so urgent? I don't know how I pulled it off but I was pulling up in front of the small café on Lenox Ave at 7:25 a.m. I had made it on time. I quickly spotted Eazy waiting for me in front of the café. Even though it was so early in the day he was still dressed to impress. This time he had on a baby blue linen pantsuit, and what appeared to be baby blue Louis Vuitton loafers. He made me feel like I was underdressed.

"Hey, glad you could make it Giselle," he said. Eazy then leaned over and kissed me on the lips. It was just a small little kiss, but I could feel the heat in my face. I knew Eazy would notice my reaction to the kiss, and this embarrassed me. I didn't know what to say or do at that point so I just stood there. After a few seconds he said, "Come on let's go order some breakfast." I followed him into the café. Eazy chose a table by the window for us. I still couldn't figure out why we were there so early in the morning. After we were seated I started looking through the breakfast menu. I didn't realize how hungry I was until my eyes scanned over the many breakfast choices. I eventually settled on the Denver omelet, and Eazy ordered French toast.

I asked, "Why are we meeting for breakfast so early in the morning?" Eazy looked at me, grinned and motioned for me to look out the window. I looked out the window and saw the sun rise over the city. It cast sunbeams in every direction, illuminating the tall buildings downtown. It was beautiful. I couldn't pull my eyes away from it. I had never actually watched the sun rise before, and I never even thought about watching it with a guy. I was grateful to Eazy for wanting me to share that moment with him. I wasn't quite sure what was going on with us. First he kissed me, and then made what appeared to be a romantic gesture. I didn't know what to think of all of this.

Eazy turned away from the window and said, "Giselle, I wanted to share this moment with you. Do you see how beautiful and breathtaking the sunrise looks? It attracts you to its beauty and you can't take your eyes away from it. Giselle that is exactly how I feel about you. This was the best way I thought I could let you know that. I feel like I'm falling in love with you. I know I have only known you for such a short time, but my feelings for you are genuine. If Friday comes and you decide to not go to California with me, I will definitely be heartbroken, but on the other hand I would have to respect your decision."

I was dumbfounded, and I really didn't know what to say. I wasn't looking for a boyfriend at this point in my life. I just needed him to help me get signed to his label. He was taking this situation into a totally different direction than where I needed to go. I just wanted to make music. Eazy sat staring at me waiting for a response, and I sat staring at my coffee because I didn't know what he was expecting me to say. I didn't feel the same way he did. This was a terribly awkward moment between us.

Eventually, I spoke up; "I'm sorry Eazy but this all sounds crazy to me. You have only known me for a few days." I looked up from my coffee and looked into his eyes. My mother always told me the eyes never lie. You can learn a lot about a person from just staring into their eyes. You can read all of their emotions. I sat there staring into

Eazy's eyes but I couldn't read him. I couldn't tell if he was genuine. It frustrated me because I didn't really know his intentions. I knew he wanted to sign me to his music label, but what else did he want? I was so confused. The next day was Thursday, and I had to have an answer for Eazy on Friday. He was going to be headed back to California on Friday, but at this point I still didn't know if I would be on that plane with him.

"Listen Eazy, I really need some time to think before I decide to go to California with you. I need to be alone right now so I can process everything. I think it's best if we don't see each other tomorrow. If I decide to go to California with you, I will meet you at the airport Friday morning. If I decide not to go I want to thank you for everything you have done," I said. Eazy's reaction was not what I expected. He looked shocked and appalled that I hadn't made my decision yet. Then he dropped his shoulders like he had been defeated and responded "Okay Giselle. I can only pray that you show up Friday morning at the airport. If not, then I will have to respect your decision," he said.

I couldn't stand to see the look of sadness on Eazy's face. I stood up and took ten dollars out of my wallet to pay for my breakfast, and a tip for the waitress. Eazy got the picture so he too stood up facing me. He gave me a hug and a quick kiss on the cheek. I then turned and walked out of the café. I looked back on my way out and Eazy was still standing at the table watching me walk away. I sat in my car and realized that I didn't want to go back home. I decided to drive uptown and visit my mother's gravesite. Maybe talking to her would help me wrap my mind around what was going on.

I sat down in the lotus position in front of my mother's angel shaped headstone. I still missed her a great deal. If she were alive I would have been able to go and talk to her, and she would have assured me that everything would be alright. She was no longer with me, so I knew I needed to make the decision on my own. I sat at my mother's gravesite and started thinking. It seemed like Eazy had a legit record label, known for signing some of the most successful artists. He was very knowledgeable and experienced in music and producing. I couldn't find anything negative about him or his label on the internet. He seemed like he was a sweet, charming guy, but the thought of going all the way to California with him still panicked me.

On the other hand, I had been singing and performing for years and this was the closest I have ever come to potentially getting a record deal. I performed everywhere in my little town and throughout the state. Everyone knew who I was, maybe I needed to relocate and take another shot at success. Maybe things would turn around for me. I had been living in my mother's house since she passed away. I thought maybe I could start to move on with my life in a positive way if I discontinued hanging on to that house. I loved the house. It sat on five acres of land. It was an old, brick Victorian style three bedroom house. It had a huge backyard. Mother had paid someone years ago to put up a privacy fence in our backyard. Under different circumstances I would have loved to make this house my home, but now it was just a constant reminder to me that she passed away in there. I even still smelled her favorite Chanel #5 perfume throughout the house. It could be rather overwhelming sometimes when I walked past her room. I had left everything as it had been when she passed away. The idea of getting rid of her things made me sad, so I left everything as it was for now.

Maybe what I needed was a new start to give me a boost of confidence. Most importantly, I made a promise to my mother to keep singing, and to keep trying to achieve my dreams of becoming a singer. I sat in front of her gravestone with all of these thoughts running through my head. Then I started to think about all the great memories. I remembered the first time she discovered I could sing. I will never forget the look of pride she had on her face. She was always my biggest fan. No one believed in me like she did.

I knew I had to keep trying for her. I had to put myself out there and take a leap of faith. I just hoped I wouldn't come crashing down and make a fool of myself. I had made my decision. I knew what I had to do. I ran my fingers across my mother's headstone and mouthed "I love you momma." Then I walked back to my car, got in, and headed home.

The next day was Thursday and I had a lot of things to do. I got in contact with a local realtor about my mom's house. I packed everything in the house up and put it in storage. She left it to me and I think it was best if I put it up for sale. I went online and I deleted all of my ads for a wedding singer and performer. I then went down to Mario's and let him know that I was moving out of town. I gave Mario a hug and thanked him for the opportunity. He told me he was sure going to miss me and whenever I'm in town, I'd always be welcome at his bar. I was sure going to miss Mario's. His customers had always showed me a great deal of love over the years.

I went home that night and packed up everything I thought I would need in California. After I packed I walked around the house. I went in and out of every room to take a mental picture of the house one last time before passing it on to another family. I had grown up there. I was sure going to miss it. But it was time for me to make a change in my life. I tossed and turned that night, and didn't get much sleep. That night I prayed to God that I was making the right decision.

The next morning, I called a cab and was on my way to the airport. I was terrified and excited at the same time. It seemed like the cab ride took forever but, in reality, the airport was only twenty minutes away. When I arrived I told the cab driver to drop me off in front. I spotted Eazy standing outside the main entry. I saw him but he hadn't seen me yet. There was a look of concern and despair on his face, and he was pacing back and forth.

The cab pulled over to the curb and I got my luggage out of the trunk. I thanked the cab driver and gave him a small tip, and then I headed over to Eazy. He still had not spotted me so I yelled his name. He turned to see who was yelling. I waved my hand in the air and he spotted me. He smiled, ran over picked me up and swung me around. "I knew you would come. I knew you'd make the right decision. I promise I won't let you down," he said. I'm glad he felt like I had made the right decision. Even though I was there to take the trip, I still was feeling a little apprehensive.

The plane ride was fantastic. Eazy had arranged for us to sit in first class. I had never even been on an airplane and now I was flying first class. I felt like I was already a celebrity. A few hours later we were landing in Los Angeles. Eazy had arranged for a limo to pick us up from the airport and take us to his house. I was bursting with excitement. I hadn't smiled this much in a long time. I was overjoyed. I knew my mother was looking down at me saying, "You made it baby, I knew you could do it." I couldn't wait to get in Eazy's recording studio. I was eager to prove to him and his partner that I had what it took to be a multi-platinum recording artist.

We arrived at Eazy's house after a short ride from the airport. I must say, I was impressed. He had a nice, modest three bedroom loft downtown. His loft was on the fifteenth floor, so he had a great view of the Los Angeles skyline from every room. The view alone was enough to take your breath away. I couldn't believe I would be waking up in a place this lavish every day. I just wished I could stay up and enjoy the night view with Eazy, but I was so emotionally drained I unpacked my suitcase and went right to sleep.

The first couple of days at Eazy's house were a little nerve-racking. I was having a hard time getting used to being away from home. Many nights I woke up and was confused about my whereabouts. I must say Eazy was as helpful as possible accommodating me in his home. He was always very charming and charismatic. He made sure I had everything I needed to make the transition as easy as possible. By week two I was doing a little better, and I was ready to get out and explore the city.

Eazy was a perfect gentleman. He treated me like a princess. He took me shopping and bought me a whole new wardrobe. Since he only took me to high end stores, I got everything from Louis Vuitton to Tom Ford. He said to me "Now that you are in Los Angeles and on your way to being a star, you have to look like one." He also bought be some really expensive pieces of diamond jewelry. I started to feel a little guilty about all the money he was spending on me so I promised him I would pay it all back when I made it big. Then he smiled at me and said, "Don't worry about it, you're my girl, and my girl has to look good." I was a little confused about that little statement. We weren't dating. I didn't think I was leading him on in any way. Maybe he just meant "his girl" as in his artist. I made a mental note to ask him about that at a later time. I didn't want to ruin our good mood that day.

Eazy had a very busy nightlife. He and I went out to some kind of party or event just about every night. People flocked to Eazy everywhere he went. It seemed like he knew everybody in Los Angeles. He always had beautiful women eyeing him. I must say I felt flattered to be the woman on his arm. He was introducing me to everyone as his girl. I still was confused about the whole couple situation, but apparently Eazy wasn't. He thought I was his girl. Eazy treated me like a lady and he had been charming since I met him, but I was still a little apprehensive about dating someone. On the other hand, he wasn't making it easy for me not to start developing feelings for him.

A few weeks had gone by and I had begun to settle into my new life in Los Angeles. The only problem was that I hadn't been in the studio yet. I had not even met Eazy's partner. I mean, that was the whole reason I came out there. I was starting to feel very anxious. I wanted to say something to Eazy about it but lately he had been so busy. I just keep telling myself that he didn't forget about me, he was just waiting until the time was right. Eazy was hardly ever at the house anymore, and when he was I barely saw him. He would come in, and change his clothes and leave back out. One day I mentioned to him that we hardly saw each other anymore. He apologized and said he had been so busy trying to close a deal.

The next day Eazy went out and bought me a two door, baby blue Lexus coupe. He said I needed to get out and enjoy the city more. Then I wouldn't feel so lonely in the house with him gone. I was so excited to have such a lavish car. I wanted to drive it all the time. Some days I would go out driving and wouldn't come back home until the sun went down. Eazy was right, I did feel a little better after getting my car. It was easier to tolerate his busy lifestyle because I was gone most of the time too.

A few weeks went by and all of a sudden Eazy was home more than usual. He stated that he had closed his deal and now had time to spend with me. He assured me that I wasn't being ignored but that I had to get use to his busy lifestyle. That week Eazy and I spent all day and all night together. I enjoyed spending time with him and I knew he enjoyed spending time with me. It seemed like everything was perfect. Before I knew it I was falling in love with Eazy. He had me on cloud nine and I loved it. The only thing still bothering me was the fact that I had not been in the studio yet.

I had gotten so frustrated and fed up about it I started questioning Eazy. He would always assure me that my time was coming and tell me I needed to be patient. I didn't understand what we needed to wait for, and when I asked him to explain it, he never would. I just needed a chance to get in that studio. I knew I had talent. I had already been in Los Angeles for three months, and was really starting to wonder if I had made a mistake coming out there.

I tried to keep myself busy and not think about how frustrated I had become. I needed something to keep me occupied, so I started writing songs. It surprisingly came easier than I thought. I was writing two to three songs a day. I regretted not trying to do something like this sooner. I could already sing. If I could write songs and sing I was a double threat. I poured all of my heart into those songs. I knew with the right beat and melody I could make the songs come to life. If Eazy would just put me in the studio already!

I was really starting to wonder about my real purpose for being there. I felt like I was wasting time, and the disappointment was growing. I didn't come all the way to California to just be Eazy's unofficial house wife. I hadn't even planned on being in a relationship with him, period. I guess I had myself to blame. I fell for his generosity and charming demeanor. I must admit, I did love Eazy but I felt I was letting myself and my mother down. I had been in California almost six months and I was starting to wonder if I should ask around Los Angeles about other producers. I didn't want Eazy to feel betrayed, but I was so frustrated. One minute everything was feeling right and then it felt like everything was going so wrong.

Then, just when I thought my situation couldn't get any worse, I discovered that Eazy was doing drugs. He started coming home really late, and sometimes not coming home at all. I thought he was just busy and working late. My mind told me not to worry, it was just his job keeping him out all night. However my heart told me it was something else. My first thought was that maybe he was seeing someone else. The last thing I expected was that he was doing drugs. One day I came home from a salon appointment earlier than expected and what I saw should have scared some sense into me. I should have left Eazy in California and never looked back, but I didn't.

As soon as I entered Eazy's house I heard voices. I was surprised that he was even home that early in the day. I was also curious as to who his company was. He hadn't brought anyone by to visit since I have lived there with him. It sounded like he had a bunch of guys with him. I heard the television and it sounded like they were watching the football game. I decided to be a good hostess and make Eazy and his friends a snack. I quickly made up some chicken salad and grabbed some cold beers out of the refrigerator and headed down the hall to the game room. The game room door was open so I didn't knock, I just walked in. What I found was beyond shocking.

My eyes naturally went to Eazy first. Then I noticed there were four other guys sitting around. One of them looked clean-cut. He had a suit on. The other three were questionable. Their clothes were rather baggy, and they had on a ton of gold chains. One of them even had a red and white scarf tied around his head like gangbangers I had seen on TV. When I looked down at the table, I noticed that each one had a line of white powder in front of them. My heart wouldn't let me believe what my eyes were seeing. I had not grown up in the heart of the ghetto like some individuals I knew, but I knew cocaine when I saw it. Everyone was looking up at me. Not shocked and surprised at all. It seemed they were just curious as to what would be my reaction. "Eazy what the hell is going on here?" I yelled. Eazy jumped up from the couch and he acted like he was confused as to what was going on. That's when I took a closer look at him. His eyes were red. "Giselle, why the hell didn't you call and tell me you were on your way home; and better yet, why the hell did you just barge in here with this shit on a tray? You should've announced that you were home, or at least knocked on the door!" Eazy yelled. "Eazy, are you doing drugs? What is wrong with you?" I asked.

One of Eazy's friends bent down and snorted up the line of cocaine laid out in front of him. He obviously didn't care if I was there or not. Then he had the nerve to say, "Eazy, look man, I know where this is going. This party is over. Let's go guys." Eazy's friends grabbed their things and headed towards the front door. I made sure I gave each and every one of them a nasty look as they exited. How dare them, they had some nerve. They all needed help, including Eazy. As soon as the last of them was out the front door, I immediately started questioning Eazy. "Eazy what is going on? I didn't come all the way to California to be with a drug addict. You need to get some help. This is not acceptable at all," I said. I started asking questions about his drug use but he wasn't even saying anything. Then he yelled at me, "Shut the hell up! I'm grown and I can do whatever the hell I want! I am taking care of you and this house and that's all you should be concerned about!"

"I can do whatever the hell I want and if that includes getting stoned, then so be it! There is a lot of shit going on with the label and I need something to take my mind off those problems for a little while, okay? So I don't want to hear anything else about this, you understand me?" I couldn't believe he was telling me to drop it. He was more insane than I had thought. This was a serious matter to me. I couldn't just drop it and pretend like what I just saw didn't happen. Eazy needed to understand that doing drugs could ruin his life and his music career.

"Eazy, I can't just drop it. It's not that simple. This is serious, you need help," I pleaded. Then Eazy started walking towards me, with a look of anger on his face. My heart started beating fast. I thought he was going to hit me, but he stopped inches away from where I stood and yelled, "Look! I said drop it, and don't think for a second that you are going to start nagging me about this or you can take your ass back to that little town I found you in!" He then grabbed his keys off the table and left the house. He slammed the front door so hard I thought all the windows in the door would shatter.

After Eazy left I went upstairs and lay across the bed and cried. I didn't understand what was happening to my life. Everything seemed so perfect. Eazy was going to ruin everything for me. I knew enough about drugs to know that if he didn't get help soon he was going to lose control and destroy his life. I had heard about all the drugs people did out in Hollywood but I never imagined I would witness it first-hand. I wondered if Eazy had been doing drugs the whole time I had known him. I knew sometimes when he came home his eyes were red and he acted strange. He would be sweating profusely, and mumbling nonsense to himself. I assumed he was just stressed out from working all the time. I never imagined he was on drugs.

I became depressed. I didn't know what to do as I couldn't depend on Eazy anymore as far as my music career. Now that I knew he was doing drugs, everything changed. I found myself not trusting him. It made me wonder if doing drugs was a regular part of Eazy's studio work. Between Eazy's drug problem and the problems they were supposedly having at the label, I felt like I would never get to record any tracks. I had all of these things running through my head as I lay there crying. All I could do was pray that things would get better, but a small part of me doubted that it would.

Eazy must have been really upset with me. Over the next couple of days he was barely at the house. When he did come home he didn't say much, and he came in stoned. I immediately knew when he came in whether he was under the influence. I had learned the signs over time. One night he came in and wanted to make love. I knew he'd been doing drugs and didn't want anything to do with him when he was in that state. He tried to kiss me and I turned my head away. He grabbed my face and forced his tongue in my mouth.

He sloppily kissed me against my will. I tried to keep from gagging because his breath was putrid. It smelled of alcohol and vomit. Once he finished kissing me he started pulling at my clothes trying to take them off. "Eazy you are stoned! Please leave me alone! I don't want to be around you when you're like this!" I pleaded. "Bullshit! You are my girl and when I want to make love to you, I can. Now take your clothes off!" he blurted. He then started pulling at my shirt, popping the buttons off as he pulled. Then he turned me around and yanked my bra off exposing my breasts to him.

Even though this was supposed to be my boyfriend and had been for months, I felt frightened, embarrassed and violated. I knew this wasn't the Eazy I had come to love. This was a drug induced maniac whom I didn't know. Eazy then started pulling and tugging at my skirt and panties. I was confused and didn't know what to do. I was his girlfriend, but should I be submissive to him under these circumstances? And if I said no would he force himself upon me anyway? Would this monster that had taken over Eazy's mind cause him to rape me? I stood in front of Eazy with my whole naked body exposed to him. He was kissing and grabbing at me everywhere. Then he started biting and nipping at my body rather painfully. I couldn't believe this was happening. Then Eazy put his mouth on my left breast and bit down on it. I screamed from the pain. I forcefully pushed him away, and he started laughing at me like it was all a big joke. "Eazy get away from me! You are high off of drugs! I don't want to be around you when you're like this!" I yelled. I reached down to pick up my clothes to put them back on, but Eazy grabbed me by my hair. It felt like he was ripping the hair out of my scalp strand by strand. "Eazy stop, you are hurting me!" I yelled.

The tears started to roll down my cheeks. He seemed unfazed by anything I was saying. He was too far gone off cocaine to care. "You will give me what is mine!" Eazy yelled. He kept my hair tangled in his hand. I tried to twist and roll my body to free my hair from his grasp but nothing I did was working. The more I tried to get loose the tighter he wrapped my hair around his fist. The pain in my head was unbearable. I stopped trying to fight him and collapsed to the ground. I held my hand in front of my face and cried. I never felt so humiliated in my life. I couldn't believe the man that I had fallen in love with was treating me like this.

Eazy looked down at me with a pitiful look in his eye. I almost thought he would just let me loose out of sympathy, but instead he started dragging me over to the bed in one of the guest bedrooms. When we reached the bed he threw me onto the bed and finally released my hair. I crawled up to the head of the bed and pulled my knees up to my chest. I didn't want him to touch me. I knew that I wasn't dealing with Eazy, I was dealing with a monster. But what could I do? He was a lot stronger than me. I was so confused. He was my boyfriend, so maybe I should just let him do what he wanted. That way it would be over quickly. "Lie down!" Eazy yelled. I looked him dead in the eyes and pleaded with him one more time "Eazy please don't do this, I don't want to be intimate with you while you are like this. I know the drugs have taken over your thoughts. It has turned you into this monster. Please don't force me to do this," I begged.

Eazy grabbed my legs from under me and forced them open. I tried to resist him and close my legs but he was too strong for me. I eventually became exhausted from trying to fight him, and my head was still pounding from him pulling my hair. I eventually became exhausted and stopped fighting. He forced my legs open as wide as they would go. I felt like there was nothing I could do at this point to stop him. I lay there silent as the tears rolled down my cheeks as Eazy had his way with me. I just prayed it would be over quick. He pounded himself into my body with such roughness and force it caused the whole bed to move.

I cried and prayed silently for it to be over. After a few more minutes went by, Eazy released himself and rolled over off of me. I heard him walk out into the living room. Then I heard him pick his keys up off the counter and leave out of the front door. In seconds, I heard his car start and he was gone. I could not believe he raped me and then discarded me like I was nothing. He acted like I meant nothing to him. He had treated me like trash in the streets, just used me and threw me away. I lay there contemplating what to do. I had just been raped by the man that was supposedly in love with me.

I didn't have anyone I could call and talk to about what happened. I knew deep down inside I should do something. It was clear I needed to leave Eazy and go back to Michigan. I was terrified to think about what might happen next time he came in high off drugs. I knew I should call the police and have him arrested, but I didn't want to see Eazy in jail. He was on drugs and he needed help. I rationalized that if he had been sober, he would have never done those things to me.

I lay there in the bed and cried. My legs hurt so badly, and I couldn't move them. The pain was so unbearable, every time I tried to get up I couldn't. I wanted to get up, wash myself up, and get Eazy's scent off of me. I closed my eyes and slowly raised myself up off the bed. I yelled and screamed in pain but was able to stand up. I leaned up against the dresser and steadied myself. I looked down at the bed and it was covered in blood.

Seeing what he had done to me caused me to start crying uncontrollably. I lost my balance and slid down the side of the dresser and onto the bedroom floor. I cried on that floor for what seemed like hours. I cried until I was emotionally exhausted. I knew I needed to get away from Eazy. I just had to wait until the right time. I eventually built up enough strength to crawl into the bathroom and over into the shower. I sat there and watched the water wash the blood from my body down the drain and wondered how my life had been turned upside down so quickly.

The next day Eazy didn't come home. I wasn't surprised at all. I didn't know if he would be on drugs or sober when he did. I had made up my mind I was leaving and going back home. He didn't come home for the next couple of days. He started sending me flowers to the house everyday. Then he started having little expensive gifts delivered to the house. He was sending expensive clothes and pieces of jewelry. There was always a note attached apologizing for hurting me. In one note, he even went on to say that he was going to check himself into rehab. I had been calling him everyday and he had not been answering any of my calls. I needed to talk to him and let him know I couldn't be bought. No amount of jewelry or clothes could erase what he had done to me, and he needed to know that.

Then all of a sudden Eazy came home. I had waited for him to set foot in the house for two weeks and now that he was standing in front of my face, I was speechless. I looked at him closely to see if I could tell whether he was under the influence. He seemed to be sober. When he started talking I knew he was not on drugs. His voice sounded like the Eazy I knew. He came over to me and tried to give me a hug and I gently pushed him away. "Listen Giselle, I'm sorry I hurt you. I was not myself that day. I had been on drugs and totally lost control. I have been over at a friend's house for the past two weeks. He has been helping me wrap my head around what I should do. I don't want to lose you or ruin my company, so next week I am going to go into rehab," Eazy said.

"Eazy are you serious?" I asked. "Yes I want you to wait for me. Please forgive me. I promise I will do my best to make it up to you. I know I brought you out here with a promise of making you a star and I'm going to fulfill that promise," he said.

I stood in front of Eazy saying nothing, I was glad that he recognized that he hurt me and that he had a problem, but I felt like our relationship would never be the same. I did feel like I couldn't leave now because I had to help him through this. I just hoped that he was able to rehabilitate himself and get his life back on track. "Eazy, I'm glad you realized you have a problem and are willing to go to rehab. I will stay out here while you are in rehab. You hurt me deeply and I'm afraid there may not be a personal relationship between us anymore. When you come out of rehab it will be strictly professional. You will be my producer and I will be your artist," I said.

The hurt look in Eazy's eyes made me feel bad for him. I understood that he was on drugs when he hurt me, but I wasn't ready to forgive him for what he had done. This was the clean sober Eazy, so I assumed that he was genuine. He knew he had messed up and there was nothing he could do about it.

The next week Eazy went into rehab and I was there to see him off. He seemed to be serious about getting clean and getting his life back on track. If he was truly serious, then I was happy for him. I stayed in Eazy's house while he was in rehab. He made sure to call me every day and give me updates on his progress. His first couple of days in there was hell because he didn't know how to deal with the withdrawal symptoms. He told me it was the hardest thing he had ever done. Eazy had opened up to me while he was in rehab more so than he ever had. I was starting to feel like he was making progress and slowly transitioning back to his old self-the Eazy I had fallen in love with.

Six months later, Eazy graduated from rehab. I was there bright and early to pick him up. As soon as he saw me he gave me a great big hug. It felt good to have the old Eazy back. I missed him. I didn't know what kind of relationship we would have, now that he was back home. Before he went into treatment I had every intention of keeping our relationship strictly professional, but it wasn't going to be as easy as I thought. During the next few days Eazy was the perfect gentleman.

He catered to my every need. He was really trying to be the man he once was for me. I appreciated his effort but I still wasn't ready to forgive, and definitely not forget, what he did. He decided to not go back to work right away. He told his partner he needed some time to relax before entering back into the music business. Eazy assured me that he and I would be spending the next two weeks together, just him and me. The next two weeks that time spent together were blissful. He treated me like a Queen. Many days he made me breakfast in bed. We did a lot of shopping. Then there were days were we just stayed in and talked while he massaged my feet. He made sure he did whatever it took to keep me happy. I guess he was really sorry for the pain he had caused me. Over those two weeks I forgot all about going back home to Michigan. I was just happy to have the man that I fell in love with back in my life.

Eazy eventually went back to work at the label, and I started writing songs again. I wanted to ask Eazy about meeting up with his partner, but I figured I would wait until he got back on his feet in the studio. Within a couple days of being back at work Eazy started going out with his friends again. I was worried about him having a relapse but I knew he had to find a way to stay clean on his own terms. Then Eazy started not coming home late at night again. I didn't want to believe he had started doing drugs again, but something happened one day that confirmed those fears and caused me to leave Eazy for good.

He came in late one night and was being rather loud downstairs. It sounded like he was bumping into furniture. When I heard a dish break I decided to go downstairs and see what was going on. The minute I saw him and that familiar look in his eyes, I knew he had relapsed. I couldn't believe after everything he had been through he would turn back to drugs. I was heart broken. If I and his career weren't enough to keep him clean, then maybe trying to help him was hopeless. I was angry at myself. I knew I should've left Eazy when I had a chance but, day after day, I chose to stay.

I became angry with myself and angry at Eazy. I was fed up. I couldn't baby sit him and make sure he stayed clean. I had to leave because this life was suffocating me. I needed to go back to Michigan. Eazy looked at me and said nothing. He turned and walked into the game room and threw his body over onto the couch. I came barging in after him and yelled, "Eazy I know you have started doing drugs again! I know you are under the influence right now! I refuse to live or be in a relationship with a drug addict! I can't be with you if this is how you are going to live. You have done nothing you promised me you would do since I got to California. You told me nothing but lies. I have been here for six months and I have not met your partner or set foot in a studio. You are a fraud! The only thing you have been doing since I've been here is party and get high. I am leaving and going back to Michigan. I will leave everything you bought me. You can have back the clothes and all the jewelry. I don't want anything from you!"

I turned to walk out of the room and Eazy jumped up off of the couch and grabbed my arm. He got right in my face and yelled," Listen you ungrateful little bitch! I brought you here and gave you a taste of the good life. If it wasn't for me you would still be back in that small ass town singing at bars and bullshit weddings!" He was so close I felt the spit on my face from his words. I was so angry. How he could think he was doing me any favors? I knew I should have just walked away from him while he was in this state, but I was so angry I had to say something.

"Don't talk to me like that! You don't have the right to talk bad about me. I came here because I believed you could help me with my career. You are nothing but a coke head and a fraud!" I yelled back at him. Then with rapid fire speed, Eazy brought his hand from behind his back and slapped me hard across the face. He slapped me so hard I lost my footing and fell onto the glass coffee table. The table shattered under me, as glass flew everywhere. Eazy then came over to where I lay and spit in my face. "You better not be in my house when I get back!" he screamed. He then grabbed his keys off the kitchen table and left.

I was stunned. No man had ever hit me before. Eazy had slapped me so hard my ear was ringing. I looked around and noticed that one of my legs was bleeding. I slowly picked myself up off the glass and went into the restroom. I started cleaning and wrapping the cut on my leg in gauze. I started to cry. I was afraid of what my face looked like but I couldn't resist looking in the mirror. What I saw was horrifying. My cheek and eye had started to swell on the right side, and my lip was busted.

I couldn't believe that Eazy had gone so far as to put his hands on me. I felt as bad as I looked. I partially blamed myself because I should have left when I had the chance. I wouldn't make that mistake again. He had raped and physically assaulted me. Giving him an opportunity for a third assault was out of the question. I limped into the bedroom and started packing up my things. I was only going to take what I brought with me. I didn't want anything that Eazy had purchased for me. I came to California with my one suitcase and I was leaving with that same suitcase. I left all the clothes, shoes, and expensive jewelry. I would show him that I didn't need him or his money. I had money of my own. Eazy always paid for everything, after I arrived in California so I still had a little bit of money in my personal account. I was going to use this money to get back to Michigan.

I finished packing my things and headed downstairs to call a cab. I sat outside on the porch with my head in my hands and cried. I felt so defeated and disappointed. I had wasted the past six months of my life, and felt like a failure. I was headed right back to where I started. Not only had I let myself down, I felt like I was letting my mother down. The cab pulled up and I walked away from Eazy's house and out of his life for good. I arrived at the airport and luckily I found a flight going out to Michigan within the hour.

I purchased my ticket and waited to board the plane. I put on my sunglasses to cover up the worst part of my face, but the looks from strangers only confirmed that the glasses did not help. I chose a seat over in a corner and waited to board the plane. Eazy had done me so wrong. I was thankful I saved the money in my personal savings account or I would've been stranded in California, with nowhere to go. Within the next half an hour I was boarding the plane back to Michigan. My flight was very upsetting and emotional. I cried the whole trip. I was just hoping I could get my life back on track and try to, somehow, begin to be happy again.

Once I arrived in Michigan, I contacted the realtor that had put my mothers' house up for sale. I needed help finding an apartment. After talking to her, I realized that since she had not found a buyer for my mother's house, I could just take my mom's house off the market and move back into it. Within the week I had settled back into the house. I went and got my things out of storage. I put my mother's belongings right back in her room just the way she left them. I immediately started looking for work. I had a little bit of money left, but I knew it wouldn't last long. I could always renew my ad in the local newspaper for wedding gigs, but I wasn't sure if I wanted to do that just yet.

The next week I received a call from a well known coffee shop downtown. They wanted me to come in for an interview the next day. I spent the rest of that evening brushing up on my resume and my interviewing skills. I felt pretty confident I would get the job. The next day I went in for an interview and surprisingly it went well. No sooner than I got back home the coffee shop was calling to offer me the cashier position. I was so grateful. I could finally start to get my life back on track. I had a roof over my head and a job. I was doing pretty well. I felt a new sense of independence.

It still made me sad to think about what had happened in California. Eazy had not even tried to contact me. It hurt me to realize that he really didn't care enough to try to make things right between us. After everything that had happened in California, I wanted to give up on having a singing career. What if the next producer turned out to be a fraud? I couldn't spend the rest of my life chasing a dream. I started to believe that maybe being a singer wasn't for everybody. I tried not to think about it too much. The whole idea of failure was depressing.

The next week I started my new job downtown and the days started to fly by. I still had not heard from Eazy. I thought about calling him just to see if he was okay, but I figured why bother if he wasn't calling to check up on me. I also didn't want to stir up any leftover feelings I had for him. I was trying to make him and California a distant memory. I had just returned from work one evening when I received a call from a number I didn't recognize. I thought it might be Eazy so I let the voicemail get it. After the beep I heard Karina's voice come over the voicemail.

"Hey Giselle its Karina, please pick up, I need you," she said. I quickly grabbed the phone before Karina hung up. "Karina, hey how are you? I'm just getting in the door from work," I said. "Hey Giselle, I was hoping I could catch you. I need a huge favor. As you know I'm getting married on Saturday. Of course you know I invited you. Anyway, the woman I was going to have sing at my wedding reception has come down with a sore throat. She had to cancel on me. I have called all over town looking for a replacement but everyone is booked. My wedding is in two days. Can you please sing at my wedding reception Giselle? I don't know who else to call," she begged

Karina was a girl I worked with at the coffee shop. She was a really sweet girl. She trained me when I started working there. We hit it off right away. We started to develop a good friendship. Every time we worked together we ate lunch at the deli nearby. One day she heard me singing to a tune on the radio when we were closing the coffee shop, and she was impressed. "Giselle, you have some real authentic talent. Have you ever thought about a singing career? My father-in-law is a music producer" she said. I didn't want to get into a conversation with her about music. Even though she was a sweet girl, I didn't want to tell anyone what had happened in California so I quickly changed the subject.

"Giselle are you still there?" Karina asked. "Yes I'm still here Karina. I'm sorry I lost my train of thought, I said. "Please Giselle, I don't know what else to do. I wanted my wedding day to be special. I don't want to be upset on my wedding day because it didn't turn out right. I will pay you double the amount I was going to pay her. I just want everything to be perfect," Karina whined. I could tell from the sound in her voice that she was on the verge of crying. I knew how much this wedding meant to her. It's all she had been talking about at work for months. I didn't want to be the one to let her down. I knew I had to help her. Besides, I would've felt so bad if I didn't.

"Okay Karina I will do it. I'll sing at your wedding. You helped me a great deal when I first started at the shop. You made me feel welcome and I am grateful to you. I'm going to sing at your wedding and you will not pay me one cent. You deserve to be happy on your wedding day," I said. Karina screamed into the phone, "Oh thank you, thank you Giselle! I owe you big time! Oh, and I don't really have a specific song for you to sing. I know you are going to sound fantastic whatever you sing so you can pick whatever love song you feel comfortable singing. I trust your judgment. Thank you again, now I can rest easy. See you Saturday," Karina said before disconnecting.

I hung up the phone and wondered what the heck I had just gotten myself into. I had not sang publicly in months, and I had two days to get my voice ready. There was no turning back now, I had already agreed to help. The day before Karina's wedding I went to my mother's graveside to think. A piece of me still felt like I had let her down. If she knew I had even considered giving up my dream of a singing career she would be disappointed. I at least owed it to her and myself to try one more time. I had one bad experience and I needed to forget about it and keep pushing. I was just so scared of being let down again. I didn't know how many times I could pick myself back up after being knocked down.

I sat in front of my mother's gravestone. "Give me strength momma. Give me strength to try again," I whispered. I sat there another few seconds and then for some reason I felt like I needed to sing. It may sound strange, but I believed if I sang at her gravesite she would hear me. I sat there and sung a few of her favorite songs. I sang songs from her favorite artists, Whitney Houston and Aretha Franklin. I could picture her sitting in front of me smiling from ear to ear. She was always so very proud of me. She was always my biggest fan. After a few more minutes I stood up and laid the daffodils on the gravesite, and proceeded down the hill back to my car.

I felt so much better after visiting her gravesite. It also felt good to be singing again. Singing made me happy and I knew I couldn't give up on it. I would be giving up on myself, and I couldn't let that happen. When I got home that evening I called Mario at his bar. I told him I was back in town, and was ready to take my Saturday set back over at the bar. "Giselle I heard you were back in town. You know my door is always open to you. I will see you Saturday night," Mario said. I got on my laptop and reactivated and polished my online ad for a wedding singer and performer.

I was ready to take another shot at this singing thing and I was going in head first. I logged off of my laptop and made me a cup of hot tea with honey. I had to make sure my voice was ready for tomorrow. I was nervous but I had found a new sense of self-confidence. I went to bed but that night I didn't think about Eazy, and I didn't feel like a failure like I had the night before. The next morning I woke up early enough to get myself ready for Karina's wedding without having to rush. I had another cup of hot tea with honey and when it was time to head over to the wedding, I was ready. Karina's ceremony was beautiful. She had everything decorated in lavender and white. Everything matched from the seat covers, to the table arrangements. I could tell she put a lot of thought and creativity into her ceremony. I was genuinely happy for her. I could only pray that one day I'd feel the same joy and happiness she was experiencing as she married the man of her dreams. I had one hour before I had to sing at Karina's reception, and I was a nervous wreck.

Karina left it up to me to pick the song I wanted to sing, so I chose to sing the song titled "So Amazing" by Luther Vandross. I loved the song and it was also one of my mother's favorite songs. I had just a few minutes before I was due to go on and sing. I still had nervous jitters. I spotted a waitress walking by with a tray of wine. I grabbed one and downed it quickly. I was hoping the wine would ease my nerves a little bit. When it was time for me to sing I said a little prayer and stepped up on the stage. When I looked into the audience, it felt like I belonged up there. It made me realize just how much I missed performing.

I belted that song out as best I could. I must say I sang that song better than anyone I had ever heard. Luther Vandross would have been proud of me that day. I did his song some serious justice. When I finished singing everyone stood and started clapping loudly. Most of the people in attendance had tears in their eyes. I had never been so proud. It was amazing how I could touch people's hearts and emotions just from sharing my voice with them. My momma was right. God had blessed me with a gift indeed. After I finished singing the reception was in full party mode. Everyone started dancing and drinking wine, and I sort of stood around and nibbled on a piece of wedding cake.

After a while of greeting her guests Karina made her way over to me. She was holding the hand of a rather attractive older man. It wasn't her new husband so I assumed it was her older brother or maybe even her father. As they approached I swallowed the piece of cake I had in my mouth and put my fork down and greeted them. "Karina the wedding was beautiful. I am so happy for you," I said. Karina then responded, "Thank you. Everything turned out wonderful thanks to you. I can't thank you enough for coming to my rescue. I don't know what I would have done without your help. You sounded absolutely amazing, and the song, my gosh Giselle, it was perfect! Speaking of your amazing talent Giselle, I want you to meet my new father-in-law Chris."

"Chris heard you up on that stage singing tonight and you blew him away. Remember, I told you he was a record producer. He lives in New York. Maybe you two can exchange phone numbers. He knows a lot of people Giselle, maybe he can pull some strings and help you record a demo, and maybe even get you signed to a record label. I will leave you two to talk about it," she said. Karina gave her father-in-law a kiss on the cheek then she left him standing in front of me. I should have been happy and jumping for joy at the fact that there was a music producer basically being dropped in my lap. Instead I was thinking, "Oh no, the last thing I need is another fake producer to sell me a dream."

Another voice was telling me I couldn't let what happened with Eazy ruin the rest of my life. If I was going to try again, now was my chance. Karina's father-in-law motioned for me to sit down. We both took a seat at one of the round tables in the back away from the reception guests. Karina's father-in-law spoke up first. He reintroduced himself to me and then asked me if I was having a good time.

I politely answered "yes" and he started talking about Karina and how he thought she was perfect for his son. As I sat and watched him talking, I noticed he had the kindest eyes I had ever seen on a man. They were a beautiful blue. They reminded me of the sky on a cloudless day.

We sat and talked for quite a while. I didn't plan on disclosing anything about my personal life to Chris but, before I knew it, I was spilling the beans on everything. Chris was just so easy to talk to. I told him all about my mother and even about Eazy. I couldn't believe I had just poured my heart out to a man I just met, but for some reason I felt comfortable in his presence. He told me about how he got into music production. He owned a studio in New York. His two children were grown and his wife had passed away three years ago from breast cancer. The more I talked to Chris the more likeable he became to me. We sat and talked until the reception was over, and then we parted ways with the promise of meeting up the next day for coffee after my shift was over.

I hugged Karina one last time and then headed home. I couldn't believe it. If I hadn't agreed to sing at Karina's wedding reception I would've never met Chris. I couldn't help but get a little excited that he was a music producer with his own studio. I didn't want to get too ahead of myself, but what if he was the real deal this time? I was so exhausted. It had been a rather long emotional day. I went to sleep that night with the sight of Chris's beautiful, kind eyes in my mind. I was actually looking forward to talking to him the next day.

The following day Chris came downtown to the coffee shop. I was delighted to see him again. I saw him come in the door, so I held up my hand and mouthed to him to give me five minutes. I finished up my shift and then went out and had a seat next to Chris. "Hello Giselle. It's good to see you again," he said. I smiled and replied, "Likewise." Chris didn't waste any time getting down to business. "Giselle, I must be honest with you, I have not heard a voice like yours in a very long time. You have got raw talent. I would be a fool to not try and talk you into letting me help you with a demo. After what you told me last night about California I felt bad for you. You are a kind, sweet girl who is just looking for an honest chance at fame. That guy Eazy you told me about took advantage of your kind heart. I know you are a little apprehensive about trying this whole music thing again, but I promise you I will not lie to you about my intentions." I would like for you to fly to New York, at your convenience of course. I want you to come when you are ready. I will not give you an ultimatum. I need you more than you need me. I want to put you in the studio immediately and start working on a demo. I know a lot of people in New York and Los Angeles that could really put your demo in the right hands if you let me help you. Do you write songs as well, Giselle?" He asked. "As a matter of fact I do, I have some with me in my purse. I keep a note-book with me so whenever I get inspired to write lyrics, I write them down right away so I don't forget. Would you like to take a peek at what I've been working on?" I asked

"Are you serious Giselle?" Chris asked with a look of shock on his face. I took the medium sized notebook out of my purse and hand-ed it to him. "Yes I do," I said. Chris sat and started looking over the songs I had been working on. I sat and drank my coffee while I watched the different expressions on his face as he read. He seemed like he was impressed with what he was reading, but then again I wasn't sure. Chris read over a few more of my songs and then he looked up at me. "Giselle these are amazing. You are amazing. These lyrics are unbelievable. You are telling your life's story in these lyrics and you do it in a way that is very unique. I would love to get you in the studio and hear you sing some of these songs. It won't be hard to find a melody for you, I'm sure you would sound great singing over anything," he said.

"So what do you say? Can you give me a chance to mold you into a superstar? You have the talent and I have the resources. I think we are on to something big," he urged. Chris sat and looked at me waiting for a reply. Honestly, I was happy and terrified at the same time. I was terrified of failure. I didn't want to get my hopes up that this was going to be my big break and then hit a brick wall. I was happy because it's not every day you are given the opportunity to potentially change your life. There was also something about Chris that made me feel comfortable trusting him. I don't know if it was because he was a lot older or if it was just the intelligence I sensed in him. I sensed that he wanted to genuinely help me. I didn't feel like he wanted anymore than that, or that he was hiding his true intentions from me. I was scared but knew I had to take a leap of faith on this decision. The next day I flew to New York with Chris. It was the best decision I ever made.

When I arrived in New York my whole world changed. Things were happening so fast it was hard to keep up. Chris arranged for me to stay at a hotel, which was fine. I wasn't comfortable staying anywhere else yet. I was thinking that maybe I would start working on my demo with Chris in a week or so, but to my surprise the second day I was in New York Chris called to tell me we were going in the studio that day. I was ecstatic, and couldn't believe it. Things were finally coming together for me.

With Chris's help we completed an awesome demo with six tracks on it. Three of the songs were my own and three were songs written by Chris's partner. Chris was true to his word. Once my demo was finished he worked night and day pushing it to the right people. A month after completing the demo, Chris managed to get one of my songs played on the radio. We chose a song I wrote titled "Never Give Up" to play on the radio. Chris was best friends with a radio personality that owed him a favor. I couldn't believe I was hearing myself on the radio. It sounded great. I was a little scared of what people would think of the song, but they loved it. People were calling into the radio station requesting my song be played again and again.

After two months of the song hitting the radio, Chris was approached by a representative from RCA records. They wanted to sign me to a three album record deal. They were one of the biggest record labels in the Unites States, and they had signed a lot of the hottest platinum recording artists. Their roster even included Aretha Franklin, Alicia Keys, and Usher. I would be crazy not to sign with them. Once I signed the contract, the label immediately went to work on my album. I was in the studio all of the time, and loved every minute of it. I still couldn't believe it. I felt like I was living a dream. Within a year of signing the contract my first album was completed. I was so proud of myself, because I had finally made it. My mother saw this vision a long time ago. She told me to never give up and that my time would come. She was absolutely right; I just wish I had her there with me to celebrate.

I sat and held my first completed album in my hand. The emotion was overwhelming and indescribable. I would not have cared if I didn't sell a single CD. I was proudly holding in my hand something that I had helped create. It gave me so much joy to see my name written across the front. I owed Chris a great deal of my success. He kept his word on everything he promised. I had much love and respect for Chris. Not once did I doubt his intentions. He told me he wanted to make me a star, and he did in every sense.

Chris threw me a huge release party for my first album. He held the party at the record label's annual ballroom. It seemed like there were a million people there. Chris introduced me to so many people that night it was unbelievable. I had a chance to meet many of the other artists that were signed to RCA. Everyone congratulated me on the album and praised my talent. I must admit it was spectacular. I was so happy and excited. I was bursting with pride. I smiled and thought to myself that this was only the beginning. I had so much more to give. I was going to ride this career as long as I could. I didn't see myself doing anything else with my life. I loved to sing. I liked how it made me feel and how it made my fans feel. I wanted to make music as long as I could.

The next week after the party was the official release date for the public. The album came out with a bang. It sold over 600,000 records in the first week alone. Chris informed me that those numbers were extremely well even for established artists. The world loved my music. Three months later Chris informed me that my album went platinum. I was so excited, I wanted to start the second album right away.

I had been writing new songs for the second album. I felt like at this point nothing could stop me.

Chris and I started working on the single for my second album. We were in the studio constantly the next week, and finished it in under a week. It was a great song I had written called "Your Worth." I wrote it when I was out in California during a very dark time in my life. It was a very emotional song, but I was proud of it. Chris and I decided to take a break from the studio after finishing the single. He asked me to meet him in his office at 8:00 a.m. the following day, and I went home to sleep. It had been a long day.

The next day I woke up early and met Chris in his office. "Hey Giselle, come on in and have a seat," he said. I took a seat across from Chris and wondered why he wanted to meet me so early in the morning. Then he spoke up, "Giselle, first off I want to say that I am extremely proud of you. I am honored to be able to say I work with you. You have achieved great success and you owe it all to yourself. You are a very talented young lady. Everyone at the label is raving about how extraordinary you are, including me. For the past year you have worked extremely hard. I don't know anyone else with the energy and determination that you possess," he stated.

"I called you in here because I want you to take a break before we continue on any further with your second album. I know you may not feel like you need a break right now, but I don't want you to get burnt out a few years down the line. You have to learn to pace yourself Giselle. It's important to take some time for yourself. Your life is getting ready to change drastically. Now that your album is certified platinum we are trying to put together your first tour. We need you to be well rested before we start your tour. Tours can be very physically exhausting for any artist. The staff and I came up with the idea of purchasing you a ticket for a relaxing cruise."

"It's on a ship called Paradise. I have heard from a few colleagues of mine that it's one of the best around. It certainly lives up to its name. We already have your reservations taken care of. I really want you to consider going and taking some time for yourself. Then when you return we'll get right back to work," Chris said. I looked at Chris and I really didn't know what to say. They want me to take a vacation? I could use the break but I didn't want to stop working on my album. I felt like if I took a break my album would be forgotten. "I know what you're thinking Giselle. Go have fun and enjoy yourself. I give you my word we'll pick up right where we left off when you return. Trust me on this," he said.

Chris then reached into the top drawer of his desk and pulled out a cruise ticket and handed it to me. I guess I could go, I thought to myself. Chris was right. He hadn't given me any reason not to trust him. We would finish my second album when I returned. I walked around to where Chris was sitting and gave him a hug. "Ok, I will go. Thank you guys, for everything. I guess I better go pack. See you when I get back," I said. Chris had scheduled for me to take a flight to Miami the next morning. Then I would board the Paradise cruise ship to begin a much needed vacation.

I didn't sleep a wink that night. I was too excited about going on the cruise. The following morning I was just as anxious as I was the night before. I boarded the flight to Miami, and then took a cab to the port. Once I arrived I was overjoyed with excitement. There were hundreds of people standing around waiting to board. I suddenly came to the realization of how far I had come. I had worked extremely hard for all of the success that was coming my way. I knew if my mother was still alive she would have been right here by my side enjoying this trip. It caused my eyes to water just thinking about how much fun we would have had. I still missed her a great deal but I knew her spirit lived on inside of me. So at that moment, I made a promise to myself to enjoy every second of life, starting with the cruise. I was not only going to do it for me, but for my mother as well.

Giselle Present Day

Boom, Boom, Boom! The crewman banged on the door and yelled, "Ma'am wake up, wake up!" He didn't get an immediate response so he banged on the door even harder. Boom, Boom, Boom!! Giselle, on the other side of the door wasn't asleep. She was listening to the soft croons of Maxwell on her headphones. She didn't immediately hear the bangs on the door. It just so happens that seconds later her CD was switching over from one song to the next. In between that three second pause she heard the banging on the door. She took her headphones off and headed to the door wondering who it could be knocking so loudly at that time of night.

"Who is there?" she asked. The crewman answered in a rather panicked tone. "Ma'am, it's the crewman of the ship! I need to talk to you. It's an emergency!" he said. "Emergency?" she thought out loud. "One second." Giselle grabbed her shirt from off of the bed, walked back to the door and removed the locks. She opened the door to find a crewman standing before her with a look of fear on his face. "What's wrong? What's going on?" she asked. "Ma'am you need to come to the upper deck immediately. There has been an accident with the ship and the captain has ordered an emergency evacuation. I need you to follow me to the upper deck immediately!" he said. "Wait a minute! What? Are you serious? I asked. "Ma'am this is a very serious matter," he said. "Okay! Oh my God. I'm coming, let me put my shoes on!" I yelled.

I quickly ran back into the room and put my shoes on, exited the room and started following the crewman to the upper deck. The closer we got to the upper deck, the crying and screaming of the other passengers became louder. We stepped onto the upper deck and it was pure pandemonium. Passengers were running around screaming with a look of horror on their faces. It felt like I had stepped into a bad movie. That's when I realized that this was absolutely serious. After seeing the realization of what was going on, I started to panic like everyone else. I started running towards the lifeboats. The passengers were pushing and shoving each other out of the way. At this point it was a fight for survival. The crew members were no help at all. They couldn't control the situation and were as scared as the passengers. There was no order to the evacuation at all. The crew members were pushing women in the waiting line over into the lifeboats.

I quickly ran over to a lifeboat and, like everyone else, fought my way to the front of the line, and like the others I was pushed into a lifeboat. There were three other young women in the lifeboat with me and they looked just as frightened and confused. "Take it down!" the crewman yelled. In an instant we were lowered down the side of the cruise ship into the pitch black Atlantic Ocean. At that moment I had never been so scared in my life. I didn't know how to wrap my mind around what was happening. One minute I was enjoying a glass of wine listening to Maxwell, and the next I was being tossed around the Atlantic in a life boat. It was enough to drive any sane person crazy.

I wondered if the crew or the captain had called for help. They couldn't just leave us out here stranded in the middle of nowhere. I was trying to stay calm and not go into a panic attack, it was like a bad nightmare that suddenly became reality. We were out there alone. We had no food or supplies, and no way to contact the outside world. I prayed help would come soon. We wouldn't survive for long under those circumstances. It was almost pitch black. The only light was coming from the ship that we had slowly drifted away from, and the dim light from the moon reflecting on the water.

I looked over at the silhouette of the cruise ship and I could tell that it was indeed sinking. It was already beginning to lean on one side. It wouldn't be long before the majority of the ship would be under water. I hoped and prayed everyone made it to a lifeboat and thanked God for sparing my life. The lifeboats were drifting away from each other. The further away we drifted from the other life-boats, the more my fears heightened. I feared that the rescuers would never find us. I felt like I was on the brink of having a breakdown. I was overcome with fear.

All sorts of thoughts started running through my head. Someone knows we are out here right? They just couldn't leave us stranded out here? Someone had to notice that a cruise ship had veered off course or hadn't checked in at the next port, right? I looked around at my pitch dark surroundings. They would never find us in the dark vastness. They probably wouldn't start searching for us until morning when we didn't show up at the next port. I just hoped we could make it that long. I started to have a panic attack and trouble breathing.

It felt like an elephant was sitting on my chest. I started gasping for air. I took deep breaths through my nose and blew out through my mouth, but it wasn't working. I knew if I didn't calm down this wouldn't end well for me. I started thinking about my mother. What would she do in a situation like this? How would she survive such a tragedy? I bet she would fight tooth and nail for her survival given the chance. My mother was no quitter. I could almost hear her saying to me "...and I didn't raise one either. Pull yourself together Giselle." She would've been right. I had come that far, which proved I was no quitter. I was going to fight for my survival. I took in a few more deep breaths and forced myself to calm down and not think negative thoughts. I just had to trust and believe that everything would be okay, and that help was on the way. My breathing started to return to normal and I was feeling a little better. I turned away from the other three women as the look of fear on their faces was no help. I scooted over to the corner of the boat and crouched down. I closed my eyes and tried to focus on something positive. I started to think about all the good times I had with my mother when she was alive. I knew memories of her would keep me calm and help me get through this, but I also prayed that help would arrive soon, or at least before it was too late.

PEACH'S STORY

I still love this gospel song. I adore it just as much today as I did the first time I heard it. It touches me spiritually in a way words can't describe. I closed my eyes and listened to the lyrics. It felt like the song touched my soul. As I sat in the front pew at church, I couldn't help but to thank the Lord for his abundant blessings. I knew my life hadn't been untroublesome, but he had been with me every step of the way. He never left my side. I am forever grateful. I felt the Lord's presence all around me, and it gave me peace.

The choir finished up the song and I opened my eyes. My husband Michael was looking over at me smiling. He knew emotionally what this song did to me. I continued to look at my husband and I couldn't help but to smile back. Michael and I had been married for six years and he still made me feel like a bashful college girl. I didn't think it was possible to love a human being as much as I love Michael. I truly felt like he was a gift from God. My husband is my soul mate and he completes me in every way. We have a bond that many people wouldn't understand. He doesn't let a day go by without telling and showing me how much he loves and appreciates everything I do for our family.

Michael has gotten me through some very tough times over the years, but we have also had a lot of joyous times over the years. He and my children mean everything to me. If our son could grow up to be half the man his father is, I would be content. I gazed down at my two children, and immediately became filled with pride. I had been blessed with twins, a girl and a boy. It's hard to believe that they would be four years old, and on their way to preschool pretty soon. The picture wasn't always so perfect for Michael and I. Before our children were born our lives had its share of joy and happiness, but also sorrow and sadness.

Had it not been for my faith and my husband I may not have made it this far. I am forever grateful to my grandmother for introducing me to my faith at a very young age. I have always tried to turn to my faith for guidance during pleasant and difficult times. I still missed my grandmother so very much. She had everything to do with the woman I turned out to be. As a kid she made it a point to teach me good old-fashioned values. As a kid my parents worked all of the time. My father worked the graveyard shift and slept all day, and my mother worked at a fabric factory during the day, and took private seamstress jobs on the side.

My parents had always been hard workers as long as I could re-member. I was an only child so I spent a lot of time at my grandmoth-er's house. I loved my parents and they loved me. They had owned their own little 1200 square foot home since before I was born. It had three bedrooms and a decent sized kitchen and living room. A lot of people thought it was small, but it was just the right size for us. We lived on a block that housed multiple families, so there were always kids outside playing around the cul-de-sac. My grandma told me my father distasted owing people so he worked hard to be able to purchase anything he wanted, and my mother became the same way over the years. They had paid off the loans on my mom's van, and my dad's pickup truck. They both worked hard to keep our little house taxes paid and food on the table. I don't remember ever wanting for anything as a kid. I always had everything I needed and a little extra.

My grandmother would pick me up after school during the week while my parents worked, and then I would spend the whole weekend with her. Then after awhile I was at my grandmother's so much I eventually just moved in with her. My parents made sure my grandmother was financially able to care for me, and my grandmother was happy to oblige. After I moved in with her she always told me that I should respect and love my parents no matter what the circumstances were because I wouldn't be here if it wasn't for them. My grandmother taught me how to dress and carry myself like a young woman, and how to conduct myself around adults.

She made sure that I addressed my elders with "yes ma'am" and "yes sir," and never to interrupt two adults while they were talking. She gave me the freedom to be a kid, but she had a way of never letting me out of her sight. Often times she would tell me, "You're a good girl Peach. You just make sure you stay away from those little young hot-headed boys. They don't want to do nothing but use you and abuse you. If you can manage that you are going to be alright." My grandmother also made sure we were in church every Sunday. If you stayed in her house you went to church. She made sure she woke me up at 9:00 a.m. sharp to make sure we made the first service at 10:30 a.m. She would tell me I had plenty of time to get dressed, comb my hair, and eat a good breakfast before we left for church.

My grandma always made homemade blueberry pancakes for breakfast every Sunday. She had been doing this as long as I could remember. She told me one day she use to make them for my father when he was a kid. I loved them. She always made sure she put a ton of blueberries in my pancakes, and I smothered them in syrup. I had never tasted anything so delectable in my life. I had tasted other blueberry pancakes but none of them even came close to tasting like the ones grandma made. I even tried making those pancakes for my own children one day. They were good but they didn't taste like my grandmother's.

After filling my belly with those pancakes on Sunday mornings, we headed out to church. We lived in a rather small town so my grandma's church was only two blocks from her house. She was never late for church! She was never late for anything. She always told me, "It's no excuse for being late, if you plan accordingly." My grandma may have been old but she had the energy of someone half of her age. I was a kid and I often times found myself running alongside her to keep up. My grandma didn't slow down for anyone either. When you were with her you either caught up or got left behind. Her sisters always teased her, saying the reason why she never married was because there wasn't a man on earth that could keep up with her. My grandma would tell her sisters, "I don't wait on anyone but the Lord."

As long as I had been alive I had never known my grandma to be late or miss a single day of church. That's how I knew something had gone terribly wrong the day I found out my parents passed away. My grandma and I had just hung up the phone with my parents a few hours before the accident happened. It was their fifteen year wedding anniversary. They both had decided to take the next morning off so my father could take my mother out for a fancy dinner downtown. Then they were going to go dancing afterwards. My mom loved to dance when she was a young girl, so my father thought it would be extra special to see her get back out on a dance floor.

That night my grandma called and congratulated the two on their anniversary. She told my father to make sure he treated my mother like the queen she is, and to make sure she has a marvelous time. Then my grandmother passed me the phone and I told my parents to have fun. My parents told me they loved me. I said, "I love you back" and then we hung up. I went to sleep that night believing that I would hear from my parents in the morning after church. I woke up the next morning, and I instantly had an uncanny feeling.

First of all, I knew it was Sunday, so why hadn't my grandmother awakened me for church? She always woke me up for church. Then I started thinking that maybe grandma overslept. I knew this was impossible because grandma was never late for church, but I didn't know what was going on. I sat up in bed and looked over at the clock on the night stand and it read 9:35 a.m. Holy cow, we were going to be late for church! I ran down the hall to my grandmother's room and threw open her bedroom door. I quickly scanned the room, but she wasn't there.

I turned and ran down the stairs and half-way down I heard my grandmother yell, "Peach stop running on those stairs before you fall and break your neck!" "Sorry grandma, but its 9:35 a.m. and we are going to be late for church. How come you didn't wake me up like you usually do?" I asked. By this time I had found grandma sitting in the kitchen. I came in and sat down across from her. She looked up at me and I immediately noticed she had tears in her eyes. I couldn't believe what I was seeing. I had never seen my grandma cry. I knew something was terribly wrong. She didn't only have tears in her eyes but she looked very somber. My grandma's eyes looked like all the life had been sucked out of them.

I had never seen her in this type of state before and it scared me. My grandmother sat there in that kitchen chair and just looked off into space. I got out of my chair and went over to her and asked, "Grandma what is wrong? Why are you crying? Are you okay?" I didn't know what else to say so I asked, "Are we going to church?" She didn't immediately answer me, which caused me to lose all composure. I didn't know what was going on but I knew it was bad. I stood in front of her and I too started to cry.

My grandma then stood up out of her chair and sat me back down. "Listen baby, grandma is okay. Sit at the table and eat your pancakes, and then we will talk. I wiped the tears from my eyes and glanced up at her as she did the same. Then she went over to the stove and brought me over a plate of blueberry pancakes. I didn't immediately start to eat, so my grandma said "Go ahead and eat Peach, I know how much you like my pancakes." I looked up at her and even though I knew she was trying to make me feel better, I still had the feeling something was wrong.

I sat at the table staring at those pancakes for a few seconds, and for the first time ever I realized I didn't want her pancakes. I wanted to know what was wrong with my grandmother. I tried again to figure out what was going on so I asked her again, "Grandma what's wrong? How come we are not going to church? We never miss church." The only response I got was "Eat your breakfast before it gets cold baby, we will talk after breakfast." I hesitated for a few more seconds and then I picked up my fork and started to eat my pancakes. I took one bite and thought to myself that these pancakes didn't taste like they usually did. It was either something wrong with me or something wrong with the pancakes.

I felt like I had no choice at this point. I knew my grandma wasn't going to let me get up from the table until I cleared that plate. I sat there and ate bite after bite of the tasteless pancakes. I eventually finished eating all of them. Once grandma saw that I had finished my food, she came over, grabbed my plate and took it over to the sink. I sat silently at the table and watched as she washed the breakfast dishes. When she finished she asked me to join her in the living room so we could talk.

As I rose from my kitchen chair I couldn't help but to wonder again what was going on. My little brain just couldn't imagine something happening so dreadful that we missed church. My grandmother took a seat in her recliner and asked me to have a seat on the couch across from her. She didn't say anything at first; she just sat there staring at me. It made me very uncomfortable. My thoughts started to take off in many directions. Then I started to think that maybe I had done something wrong. I had always been so well behaved. I couldn't think of anything I had done that would make her so sad and bring her to the point of tears.

Finally, when I started nervously biting on my pajama sleeve grandma finally spoke up. What she would tell me that day would change my life forever. Grandma sat up in her recliner, looked me in my eyes, and finally told me what had happened. "Peach your parents were on their way back from a reggae club last night and they were involved in a terrible accident. A semi-truck driver fell asleep and crossed the median on the highway. The truck hit your parents' car head on, and they died from the impact." Then she went on to tell me something about God and heaven and angels but at that point I was only half listening.

I sat there staring at my grandma. I was in shock. I saw her lips moving and knew she was talking to me, but I couldn't comprehend her words. The only thing running through my mind at the time was "I'm ten years old and my mom and dad have just been killed." I didn't want this kind of life. Why was this happening to me? I had never done anything bad in my life. I didn't deserve for this to be happening to me. I didn't want to be the kid at school that everyone felt sorry for. It reminded me of Brittany, a classmate of mine. Her father was killed in Iraq.

Brittany cried and cried in class every day. The teacher would send her to our counselor Mrs. Shavaughn on a regular basis. The other adults were always hugging her and saying how sorry they were for her loss. I felt so bad for the girl, but I never said a word to her. I sat there in my grandma's living room and wondered if now I would be that girl that everyone would feel sorry for. I didn't want to be that person. I didn't want adults in my face telling me how sorry they were. I didn't want anybody to feel sorry for me. I started crying as I sat there and thought about all of the miserable days I had ahead of me.

My grandma came over to me and wrapped me in her arms. She started to rock me in her arms and told me everything was going to be okay. I looked up and told my grandma that I didn't want to go to my parents' funeral. She knew I was petrified of going to funerals. I had developed a severe fear of funerals when I was just a young girl, just barely four years old. My mother's brother Charlie smoked cigarettes. He was what most would call a chain smoker. He was diagnosed with lung cancer, and would eventually pass away from it. My mother brought me to his funeral, and it was devastating. I knew my uncle had passed, but I still couldn't wrap my young mind around exactly what happened. I just remember everyone crying and moaning. I didn't know what to do, or how to react. I became upset, and started crying also. My mother tried to console me, but at that point my young mind had been devastated. From that point on I have always avoided funerals. My grandma was aware of this so she looked down at me and said "It's okay Peach, I'm not going to make you go. I want you to remember your parents as being good people and not laying in a casket."

I stayed home from school on Monday. My grandma and I sat around and looked at old pictures of my parents. I thought looking at pictures would make me sad but it actually made me feel a little better. I knew it was going to be a long time before I would be mentally okay without them in my life. But like my grandma told me, I had to take it one day at a time. I told my grandma I wanted to go back to school the next day, and she said if I felt ok I could go. I lay in bed that night and came up with a plan. I decided that I wasn't going to talk to anyone. Not my teachers, or the other kids or the school counselor. The only person I was going to talk to was my grandma. She was the only one that could make me feel better when the mourning became overwhelming.

If I got to school and I felt like I wanted to cry, I wouldn't do it. I was going to show no emotion in front of those people. I went to school the next day and was totally mute. I became a wall of steel. My prediction of what everyone's reaction would be was as accurate as it could get. Everyone was in my face telling me how sorry they were, and wanting to give me a hug. This just made the situation worse. I guess I just had a different way of grieving than everyone else.

I went the whole day without saying a word to anyone. If I kept this up I was hoping they would eventually leave me alone. When I got home from school that day I immediately went into the kitchen and found my grandma. She took one look at me and I started to cry. I didn't need to tell her. She knew I would have a tough time at school that day. She wrapped me in a bear hug and I told her everything that had happened at school. I had not talked at school all day, so I sat and talked to my grandma all evening. By the end of the evening I felt a lot better. My grandma always knew what to say to make me feel better.

I continued to go to school and not speak to anyone. I made sure I did my class work and homework but I still didn't speak to anyone. My teachers assumed I was grieving my parents' death and that I would eventually come around in a week or so. The days started to turn into weeks and the weeks turned into months. My teachers became worried about me because I still wasn't communicating with anyone. One evening the school counselor called my grandma and recommended that she take me to see a psychologist.

I was in the kitchen when my grandma took the call and boy was she upset. I heard her yell into the phone, "No grandchild of mine is going to see a shrink. She lost her parents for God's sake! As long as she's doing her school work correctly and not harming herself or others, we don't need a doctor getting in our business!" Then my grandma slammed the phone down on the cradle. Those people at my school hounded my grandma so bad that she took me out of school. I didn't realize how bad the school was hassling her until one day I got home and she informed me that I wouldn't go back.

She told me that I would be home schooled from now on. We went and bought the materials that day. The school personnel weren't too thrilled about my grandma taking me out of school, but I on the other hand was extremely happy with her decision. With the materials she purchased, she started home schooling me right away. She started making me blueberry pancakes every morning before I started my studies, and they began to taste very good, like the way I remembered them. I wasn't missing school one bit.

I still had bad days when I thought about my parents and how I missed them. These episodes would sometimes lead to tears, but my grandma was always there to console me and make me feel like everything was going to be okay. My grandma and I got right back into our routine of going to church every Sunday. I was getting older and the conversations I was having with my grandma was changing. She started talking in a more mature fashion. She started talking to me more and more about my educational goals, and how I should be treated and respected as a young woman.

Then one evening my grandma and I were talking when our conversation started to go in a different direction. We were talking about which college I would attend when she told me, "Peach I have these talks with you because I want you to be prepared mentally for whatever situation may come your way. One day I'm going to go be with the Lord and I need you to be able to look out for yourself." I had mixed feelings about what she was telling me. I knew as a young woman I needed some guidance but I didn't want to think about my grandma not being by my side. I felt like she was the only person I had left that I could talk to.

The months flew by, and with my grandma home schooling me, I excelled very rapidly. I knew I would get out what I put into it. I started to study hard and complete the assignments at a very rapid pace. Before I knew it I was able to take the exams for my high school diploma. I wasn't nervous because I knew I had studied hard. It paid off because I passed my exams with flying colors. Two weeks later I took my SAT exam and I received an exceptionally high score on those also. My grandma was so proud of me and I was proud of myself. I had come a long way under unfortunate circumstances.

I knew I was going to go to college, it was just a matter of which one. That fall I applied at University of Virginia.. I was a very well known university throughout the United States. I wanted to enroll in their Human Resources and Management program. I was on pins and needles the next two weeks, waiting to hear from the school. Finally, three weeks later the letter came. I had my grandma open it and tell me what it said. She tore the letter open and stared at it for a few seconds. I knew she was reading it silently to herself. "Grandma, what does it say?" I asked. She put the letter down on the table and she smiled at me and said, "Peach, it says you need to pack your bags, you are a college girl now." I screamed and started jumping up and down all over the house.

My grandma came over to me and gave me a big hug. "I knew you could do it Peach. I knew you could do it all along," she said. I couldn't help but think that everything was finally working out for me. I had lost my parents but I didn't lose my perseverance to succeed. I was going to a college that I could be proud to display on any wall. The university was only thirty minutes away from my grandma so I could still see her quite a bit. I knew my grandma was proud of me and my accomplishments. I was most proud of being able to make her happy. She had done so much for me already and I was forever grateful.

I was excited about starting college and nervous about starting this new journey into adulthood. I had been with my grandma for so long, and I knew I'd be among people of my same age in the real world. I knew my grandma had my back and so did God. I had to believe with those two I would be alright. The following fall my grandma and I drove up to the university to bring my things I would need for my dorm. My parents had left me a respectable amount of money in their insurance policy, so I was going to live on campus.

I had one other young lady who shared the dorm room with me. Her name was Farina. She had just arrived to the states from Africa, on an educational Visa. My grandma and I introduced ourselves to the young lady. She instantly made my grandma and I comfortable. I got the feeling that she was a fairly likeable individual. We put all of my things away and my grandma pulled out of her purse the bible that she usually keeps on her sofa table at home. She slid it in my top drawer and told me "Don't forget to read yourself a scripture every night before you go to bed. I am here for you and the Lord is too. All you have to do is call on him and he will answer," she said. She came over and gave me a hug and whispered in my ear, "I'm so proud of you Peach." It was enough to make my eyes start watering.

"Now don't you start that crying" she said. She gave me one last squeeze and headed towards the door. I walked her down the stairs and then watched her climb into her car. I motioned for her to roll the window down and I told her "Call me when you make it home grandma. I love you." She blew me a kiss and promised to call and then she was gone up the road. I watched her car until I couldn't see it anymore. Then I turned and went back into the dorm.

I quickly wiped the tears that had started descending from my eyes and started unpacking more of my clothes. I had to take that moment to remind myself that I would be seeing grandma for Thanksgiving.

If I needed her she was only thirty minutes away. For some reason I felt like if I said that often enough the time would go faster. My grandma called me that night as promised. She once again reminded me how proud she was of me. She told me she knew that my parents would be proud of me also. I began to feel better about making this new transition in my life. I knew I had come a long way, and I was determined to be successful.

After I hung up with my grandma, I lay in bed thinking what the next few days, and even months would bring. Once I got familiar to my surroundings and became accustomed to my classes, the transition from being under my grandma's roof to being a college student was smoother than I thought. The days were flying and before I knew it I was studying for my end of first semester exams. My grandma continued to call me every night like usual. That Friday night I was talking to her on the phone and she asked me if I was nervous about taking my exams. I reassured her that I had been doing a great deal of studying and I was confident I would do okay. My grandma laughed and then she said, "That's my girl." It made me smile because I could actually picture her lying in bed with her bonnet on smiling. Her words of encouragement always warmed my soul.

The next four days I studied like crazy. I didn't have much of a social life so most of the time I would go to the campus café and study. It was by far my favorite place on campus. I loved the atmosphere of the little café. It had more of a peaceful intimate feel. It wasn't turned-up and rowdy like most places on campus. It was a great place to study. Most of the students who came there kept their heads buried in textbooks or on their laptop screens. I had fallen in love with their peach green tea. I was there so much, most of the waiters knew me. They had become accustomed to automatically bringing me my favorite tea when I arrived. I usually sat in there most of the evening studying for my exams. By the middle of the week I decided to give myself a break. I decided to visit one of the popular pizza hangouts on campus. I didn't socialize much but I sat in the booth in the back and watched the college kids go in and out.

THE GOOD THE BAD THE UGLY AND THE BEAUTIFUL

I ordered a soda and took in the scene. My mind started to wonder about what my grandma was doing. She had not called me the night before. She knew I would be cramming this week so she probably didn't want to disturb me. It was still rather unsettling to me that she hadn't called. I grabbed my cell phone out of my book bag and dialed my grandmas' number. My grandma didn't answer the phone, it just rung and rung. I hung up and dialed her number again and still no answer. I got up from the booth at the pizza parlor and headed home.

I was starting to really worry about my grandma. I was on the verge of having a panic attack. I hoped and prayed she was okay. This was unlike her to not call me before bed, or not answer her phone. I started to think that maybe I should drive over to her house. I knew I had exams in two days, but I wanted to know what was going on. All of these things were running through my mind. I did know that if I showed up at her house this late at night and she was okay, she would most certainly tell me about myself. She would tell me I had no business leaving the campus when I should be there studying for my exams.

After I weighed the pros and cons of leaving campus I decided to not drive down to my grandmas'. I did decide to read a few scriptures from my grandmas' bible to calm my nerves. I read that bible for about an hour, and then I slid it back in my top drawer. I was sleepy, but I made sure I stayed awake long enough to say my prayers. I asked God to watch over me and my grandma, and then I went to sleep.

The next morning my cell phone started ringing very piercing in my ear. I thought I was still dreaming so I didn't immediately pick it up to answer it. It stopped but a few seconds later someone was calling me again. Who in the heck could be calling me at 6:00 a.m. in the morning? Then my mind went back to my grandma. She was calling me back. I quickly picked up my cell phone and answered it. "Hello grandma," I said. Then I heard a voice respond back, "No Peach, it's not your grandma, it's your aunt Gloria." I wondered what my aunt Gloria would be doing calling me this early. I hadn't talked to her since my parents passed away.

I also wondered why she was calling me from my grandmas' house."I'm sorry. Hi Aunt Gloria," I said. Then my auntie went on to say, "Listen Peach your grandma had a heart attack yesterday morning. The cleaning lady found her when she arrived to clean this morning. I'm sorry Peach. When she found her, she had passed away. We are planning to have a funeral within the next few days," she said. I sat frozen on the other end of the phone. I heard what my auntie was saying but was voiceless. I couldn't comprehend or believe what she was telling me.

My grandmother was dead. How is that even possible? How could she have had a heart attack? My grandma was healthier that most people half her age. Was she telling me the only person I had left who I cared about is dead? First my parents passed away, and now my grandma had passed away also. I heard my aunt calling my name into the phone but I couldn't answer her. I hung up the phone and threw it against my dorm room wall. My life was over. At that moment I didn't know how I would live without my grandma. I collapsed onto the floor and I began to cry like I had never cried before. I had never experienced a misery like I was feeling now. I didn't know what I should do. I had exams in the morning and I needed to hear my grandmas' voice tonight to tell me how proud she was of me. I couldn't think of anything to do except cry.

I stayed on that floor and I cried all day long. I couldn't move. I was so full of grief from the loss of my grandma. I didn't get up to do anything. I didn't eat, drink, or even study. The only thing I could do was cry. I felt like crying until I couldn't cry anymore. I was heartbroken. My roommate came home and saw me crying on the floor. She brought me a pillow and laid it under my head and walked back out the door. I know she wondered what was wrong, but I couldn't bring myself to tell her I had lost the most essential person in my life.

I had made it through the storm and come this far because of my grandma. Now I didn't have anybody to even help me get through her death. I lay on that floor all evening and into the night. My mind was numb and so was my body. My heart was totally crippled. I asked God why he had taken someone so important away from me. Didn't he see that she was all I had and I needed her in my life? Why would I have to be subjected to so much sorrow right now? I began to really feel like I was in a dark place. I wished my heart would just stop beating at that moment, so I could be united with my grandmother in heaven.

At that moment I didn't even see the purpose of continuing my education. I didn't really care anymore. My grandma wouldn't be here to see me accept my masters degree so I thought to myself, "What's the point?" I was really thinking about just dropping out of school. My grandma was my biggest motivation for success. I had cried so much that now I was struggling to stay awake. I was physically and mentally drained. I got up off the floor and climbed into bed and practically passed out. Three hours later my alarm clock was waking me up. I didn't want to get up. I wanted to just lie in bed, be heavyhearted and say "fuck everything." I was still contemplating just dropping out. Then I started to think about where I would go and what would I do?

My grandma always told me that education was the key to success, and that I wouldn't get far without one. I started to feel bad because I knew my grandma would be disappointed in me if I dropped out of school. I didn't want everything she did for me to be for nothing. I took a deep breath and then climbed out of bed. My eyes went over to my top drawer and I thought about my grandmas' bible I had in there. I remembered her saying to me that she and God would be there for me if I needed them. All I had to do was call on them. I got down on my knees and I began to pray "Dear Lord, please give me the strength to go on without my grandma. She has always been my motivation to succeed. I'm not sure at this point how my life can ever be contented again without her here. I am feeling very depressed and hopeless right now. Please help me to understand that you needed her more than I did. Please help me to keep my faith and try to understand that everything happens for a reason. Amen"

After I finished praying, I was feeling well enough to get myself up and get ready to go take my exams. I still felt numb. I didn't want to go out in public. I felt like everyone would know what I was going through, and how I felt. I made it to all of my classes on time, and I was able to finish all of my exams. I wasn't sure how I did. I just know I answered the questions to the best of my ability. I knew my grandma would have been proud of me, so that made me feel okay. Over the next two days I waited anxiously to find out if I had passed my exams or not. Then by day three the faculty sent out emails to the students, letting them know our grades were posted.

In spite of everything I was going through with my grandmas' passing, I managed to ace all of my exams. I couldn't do anything but smile. I looked up at the sky and mouthed," Thank you Lord."

I decided that I did not want to attend my grandmas' funeral. Just like when my parents passed away, I would say goodbye in my own way. I wanted to remember my grandma alive and well. I also decided not to go home for Thanksgiving. I wasn't close to any of my family anyway, so I figured I wouldn't be missing anyone or anything. When the start of the next semester approached I threw myself into my studies more diligently than before. I was back to doing my homework and studying at the campus café.

That little café was really becoming my home away from home. I knew all of the cashiers by name now, and even what shifts they worked. A few of the girls tried to invite me to campus parties and other social events but I always turned them down. After awhile they just quit asking. They just assumed I didn't have or care for much of a social life.

Then one evening I was sitting in the café studying. I had my face buried in one of my textbooks, when I noticed a shadow standing over me. I glanced up and saw a tall and rather nerdy looking young man staring down at me. From first glance he looked like a loner to me, but he was attractive. He was very well dressed. He wore a white polo and khakis. He also had on what looked like a brand new pair of Footjoy golf shoes. My Granddad was a golfer and I remember him wearing those same shoes when I was a kid, so I immediately knew what they were. He looked like he was going to play golf at an exclusive country club. He looked a little out of place in the campus café. I just stared, I didn't say a word. I thought to myself; this is my table I don't have to talk to him. He saw that I wasn't saying anything so he looked at me and said, "Hello young lady. My name is Michael. Do you mind if I have a seat across from you? I see you in here alone a lot. You look like you could use a friend or at least a study partner."

I didn't say a word to him, I just pulled out the seat across from me and he got the idea. I immediately didn't feel comfortable with him invading my space. He was nice looking but I wanted to look at everything but him. I started looking down at my books and then looking around at the waitresses in the café. They were all looking at me funny like they knew I was uncomfortable with this guy being over here. A couple of the waitresses even started snickering at me. I looked back at them and cut my eyes at each of them. This was not funny. I was starting to feel embarrassed by my awkwardness.

I sat and continued to try to study. I decided that I would just ignore him. When he noticed that I wasn't paying him any attention he would eventually just get up and leave. He seemed like he was rather comfortable in that chair across from me. He would occasionally look at me and smile. I must admit his smile tugged at my heart strings. His smile brightened his whole face. He would easily be considered charming to most women, but I wasn't trying to look at him like that. He reminded me of the actor Taye Diggs. Having a boyfriend or dating was the last thing on my mind right now.

After sitting across from each other and not talking he decided to open his mouth. I heard what he was saying but I was too apprehensive to look him in the eye. He didn't care that I wasn't looking at him. He went on to tell me about how he's majoring in Business Administration, and how he wanted to have his own business one day. He told me about his family, and how many siblings he had. I sat and looked up every few minutes but I didn't have the nerve to talk to him. We both sat there until after supper time. Then he packed up his books and stood up and said, "Have a nice night, it was nice meeting you," and then he walked out of the café.

I packed up my things and then headed back to my own dorm. I arrived back at my dorm room and took a bath and climbed into bed.

I kept trying to convince myself that I was not interested in Michael. I tried to force myself to think about something else, but my mind kept wandering back to him. I didn't matter either way. I probably wouldn't see him again. I was absolutely wrong about that. The next day I was back in my usual spot at the café. I had been in the café for about ten minutes when in walks Michael. Don't you know he walked his little skinny behind right over to my table and had a seat like we were old friends? I'm sure I looked like a total fool because I was sitting there with my mouth hanging open. I was in total disbelief.

Michael unpacked his books and then said to me, "Good morning beautiful, you know I thought about you a lot last night. Even though you have not said a single word to me, I yearn to be in your presence. I feel like there is something very special about you." I didn't respond to him. I sat and stared at him. There was no way in the world I was going to tell him I also thought about him last night. He looked at me a second, and then went on rambling about his family and where he wanted to be academically before the end of the semester. I had to admit he seemed pretty intelligent and serious about his schooling.

I found myself slowly becoming a little more comfortable around him. I still wouldn't speak to him but I started looking up at him more. When he started packing his books up, I felt rather disappointed. I couldn't believe how time had gotten away from us. I felt like he had just sat down. I slowly started to pack up my things as well. He threw his book bag over his shoulder and told me good evening and then he was gone. I watched him walk away and then I slowly made my way back to my own dorm. I had the weirdest feeling about Michael. When he sat and talked to me it reminded me of the talks I use to have with my grandma.

I really wanted to talk to him and get to know him better, but the truth is I was scared to get close to anyone in fear that I would lose them. It seemed like everyone I had really loved had passed away. I know I needed to make some changes in my life. I didn't want to always be a depressed individual. I wanted a life. I had dreams of marrying my prince charming and having kids just like every other woman.

Those dreams were now scaring me because the Prince Charming in my dreams now had Michael's face on them. I was okay with the anti-social life I was living. Michael had come into my life and threw me for a loop. I just didn't think I could handle disappointment. I had experienced so much hurt and disappointment in my young life already. I didn't know what I should do, but once again I fell asleep with Michael on my mind.

The next day, like clockwork, I headed over to the cafe. When Michael came strolling in I couldn't help but smile. I was ashamed to admit to myself that now I looked forward to seeing him come strolling into that café every day. I was getting used to his company. He quickly took his seat and said hello, and this time I at least smiled at him. Now I could be wrong, but I could have sworn I saw a twinkle in his eye when I smiled at him. He smiled back and then started telling me about a rather important group project he was working on. Like before he talked on into the evening hours. I knew he would need to leave soon and I didn't want him to go. He looked at his watch and then he started packing up his things. He said good bye and I smiled at him and we parted ways. I hated to see him go but I knew he would be back tomorrow.

I was so physically and emotionally drained when I got back to my dorm. I went straight to bed. I didn't have time to stay up and think about anything. The weirdest thing happened that night. My grandma came to me in my dreams. She looked just like how I remembered her. She looked so content and peaceful. I kept calling out to her and trying to touch her. The closer I got the further she floated away from me. Then she stopped and she stood before me and said, "Peach you need to learn to be happy again. You have to learn to live. You are getting in the way of your own happiness. I'm in a better place and I'm okay. It's time for you to take a chance Peach. You deserve to be happy." I nodded and then she disappeared. I was thinking to myself that I knew exactly what she was talking about.

The next morning I woke up feeling like all my burdens had been dissipated. I knew what I had to do. I was scared and I was excited. It was time for me to start living. I was going to turn over a new leaf. I ate breakfast and then went for a quick jog to clear my mind. When I finished my run I made my way over to the campus café. I took my usual seat in the back and waited for Michael to walk in. My heart was beating so rapid as I sat and waited for him. I felt like it would beat right out of my chest. I needed to get a hold of my emotions before I made a fool of myself. Then I looked up and he was coming towards me.

"Hello again beautiful, it's good to see you again," he said. He looked at me with those kind eyes and that dazzling smile of his and all of a sudden I wasn't nervous anymore. I knew I needed to give this man a chance. I may never meet another man like Michael. At that moment I thought about the advice my grandma had given me. Michael was use to me not responding to him so he pulled up a chair and sat down like he always does. I closed my eyes and said a quick prayer. When I open them Michael was looking at me. Okay I thought, it's now or never so I looked Michael in the eyes and said, "Hello Michael, my name is Natasha but everyone calls me Peach."

Michael sat and the expression on his face made him look like a deer in headlights. I knew he was astonished that I had spoken to him. Then he looked at me with the biggest smile on his face. This made me laugh because for once he was the one speechless. We both sat and looked at each other and then Michael started talking. But this time I talked back. It was a little strange at first, but after a few minutes we were talking like old friends. From that day forward we never left each other's side. We were inseparable.

I thank God everyday for bringing Michael into my life. We both went on to graduate from college with honors. Michael received his Masters degree in Business Administration and I received my Bachelors degree in Human Resources Management. We married as soon as we both graduated. It was a beautiful intimate wedding. We decided to get married at our favorite spot. There was a big beautiful oak tree down by the lake behind the college campus. It was the perfect setting for our fall ceremony. The leaves had already started to change colors. Quite a few of them had already fallen around the lake. We spent a lot of time down by that tree because it was such a peaceful spot by the water. We both thought it was only right to get married at that exact location. I just wished my parents and my grandma could have been there to celebrate with us. Even though they weren't there physically I knew they were looking down at us.

Michael was a very family oriented man. His family was very important to him. He invited all of his family to take part in our special day. I had been introduced to most of them when we were in college, and I loved them like my own. I had lost contact with my own family after my parents passed away, and no one bothered to try to contact me after my grandma's funeral. Michael and I spent a week in Puerto Rico for our honeymoon. I had never had so much fun in my life. We swam in the ever-popular La Mina falls. Learned how to salsa. I discovered that Michael has some pretty good rhythm. We walked on the beach and watched the sun set every night. It was a great week. I was grateful that I could spend it with the love of my life.

After Michael and I came back from our honeymoon we moved into our new home. It was a beautiful three bedroom ranch style home. The backyard was big enough for a nice sized pool. I had my dream kitchen. It was huge, with an island right in the center. It also had his and hers closets, and a huge whirlpool tub in the master bedroom. I adored our new home. It was the perfect size. We had already been talking about starting a family before we were married so we wanted to make sure we had room for one.

I was a little anxious about the thought of children. I didn't have any experience at all with kids, since I was an only child. Michael assured me that we would have all the help and guidance we needed from his family. He continuously told me not to worry, so I didn't. The following summer after we moved into our new home I noticed that I had missed my period. At first I was in denial. I kept telling myself that maybe it was just late. When two days late turned into a month I knew something was up. I took a test and it came back positive.

Three months into my pregnancy Michael and I had also found out we didn't have just one little blessing, but two. Michael was so excited. I had never seen another human so happy. I was a little nervous but I knew I would be okay with Michael's support. Two months after that I went in for a sonogram and we found out we were having a girl and a boy. I couldn't believe how blessed we were. It sometimes made me sad because I knew my parents would never get to meet their grandchildren, and my grandma would never get to hold her great grandchild. I knew I had to just trust and believe that they were looking down on us receiving all of these wonderful blessings.

I carried my twin's almost full term. They were born on Valentine's Day. Michael was so excited to be a daddy. He was so proud of what we had created. They were the most beautiful babies I had ever seen. They both had Michael's hazel colored eyes, and a head full of black curly hair. I was a little nervous about bringing them home at first, but I had Michael's mom there helping me out. Michael, on the other hand, was amazing with the babies from day one. He had helped raise his younger siblings so he knew a lot about caring for a baby. He never seemed to get exhausted or worn out like I did. It seemed like from the time I brought them home, I spent every waking hour with them.

Days would fly by and I wouldn't even realize it. Michael's mom still came over frequently but for the most part I was caring for them until Michael came home from work. I was determined to be a good mother, so several emotional "breakdowns" and lots of prayers later, I developed a routine when caring for the twins. It became a lot easier for me after that. It was amazing how time flew by.

Those days were over quick. The twins grew up and they are now four years old. They would be starting preschool in the fall. I decided to go back to work part-time. I didn't want to overwhelm myself with work, so I could still spend time with the kids. Michael and I were still crazy in love with each other. We had just recently celebrated our five year wedding anniversary. It had been a long road for both of us and definitely an experience being a young married couple in love, but I wouldn't change a thing. He was still the same man I married five years ago. Michael's mother watched the kids and we went out for a romantic night on the town to celebrate. Michael surprised me that night with a ticket for a seven day cruise. It was for the Paradise cruise ship.

I had heard about this ship and how extravagant it was. I asked Michael why he only gave me one ticket and he said I was the only one going. He told me it was time for me to cater to myself and not be worried about him or the children. He thought I needed a vacation. He told me I deserved it. I deserved a little free time away from him and the kids. I was a little unsure at first but the more I thought about it, the more I liked the idea. It sounded like it could be lots of fun. I knew I would miss my husband and my kids, but honestly I needed a vacation before I went back to work. I tied up some loose ends with my house, and made sure the kids had everything they needed before I left. A week later I was boarding the Paradise cruise ship. By this point I had become more and more excited about the idea of this vacation. I was looking forward to having a great time.

Peach Present Day

Boom, Boom, Boom! "Ma'am open up, there has been an emergency!" the crew man yelled. I rolled over in bed and mumbled "Michael check on the kids honey. It sounds like one of them is yelling." Then I heard it again; BOOM, BOOM, BOOM! This time I opened my eyes and I realized where I was. I was on the cruise ship. I wondered what the heck they wanted at this time of night. I rolled over and turned the lamp on and looked around the room.

I got out of bed and put my slippers on. I went over to the door and open it and there stood one of the ship's crewmen. "Can I help you sir?" I asked. "Ma'am, there has been a terrible accident with the ship. The captain has ordered an emergency evacuation. We need you to get dressed right away and come above deck. You need to be escorted onto a lifeboat immediately," he said. I stood looking at him like he was insane. "I'm sorry, is this some kind of sick joke?" I asked.

"No ma'am, this is no joke. This ship is sinking you must hurry," he said.

After he said that I threw on my clothes and shoes and ran out the door behind the crewman. Once we got to the upper deck it was total chaos. There were passengers screaming, wailing, pushing and running everywhere. That's when I realized this was no joke, this was for real. It looked like something you would see in a bad documentary. The crewmembers were trying to keep some kind of order but it wasn't working.

I was standing there observing everything going on around me. I just couldn't believe it. I was in shock. I didn't know what I should do. So I went over to the lifeboats and in an instant I was practically pushed over into one of them. I landed hard on my elbow. There were three other women in the boat with me. They looked a lot younger than I. They all looked just as scared and confused as me. We felt the lifeboat being lowered down the side of the ship and into the ocean. With every jerk I felt from that lifeboat being lowered down, I gasped for air. I literally felt like the air had been sucked from my lungs. The realization of what was going on was really starting to hit me, like a ton of bricks.

I started thinking; "We are out here in this lifeboat in the Atlantic Ocean in the middle of nowhere. We could very well die out here before anyone got a chance to rescue us." I didn't want to die. I wasn't ready to leave my family. I had two children and a husband at home I had to get back to. Someone was looking for us, right? They had to be, they couldn't just leave us out here. I couldn't let my children grow up without their mother. I didn't want them to feel the hurt I felt when I lost my parents at a young age.

I had to just calm my nerves. Sure we would get rescued. We had to try and stay calm and wait for help. What would Michael think if I didn't return? After all, he is the one that bought me the ticket for the cruise. He would feel horrible. He would blame himself for my death. I knew I shouldn't be thinking these things but I was terrified. I decided at that moment I wouldn't think the worse of our situation.

I had to keep my faith strong. I had to believe that God would see me through this. I closed my eyes and I started to pray. If I made it out of this situation I would be forever grateful to the Lord for sparing my life. And if the unthinkable happened, I would be praying until my last breath.

SOS

The sun had begun to rise over the Atlantic Ocean. The pitch black night slowly started transitioning into day. The ladies had all fallen asleep in each of the corners of the open boat during the night. The brightness and blazing heat of the sun was now causing them one by one to awaken and open their eyes. As each one opened her eyes there was a look of shock and disappointment on her face as they became aware of their surroundings. They all realized the same thing. They were indeed still living the nightmare they had witnessed just hours before. They had been stranded for nine hours in the ocean. The ladies had no watches or phones, so they had no perception of the amount of time that had passed. The nine hours easily felt like nineteen hours.

They each pulled themselves up into a sitting position and searched the water and sky for any sign of a rescue boat or plane. There were no signs of anyone or anything in the water except them. After a few minutes of straining their eyes: Peach and Jewel averted their eyes away from the ocean. Jackie and Giselle continued to search the ocean for any little sign of a rescue boat. Peach leaned up against the corner of the lifeboat and closed her eyes. No one spoke but the same thoughts were on all of their minds. They couldn't believe no one had come for them yet. They were relieved that they had made it through the night, but worried because they had not been rescued.

Jewel wondered if the rescuers had come looking for them during the night, but because they were asleep they had failed to get the rescuers' attention. They all felt a high level of anxiety. They were alone and vulnerable in the ocean. They didn't have anything to protect themselves should trouble arise. All they had was each other at that point.

Peach sat up and opened her eyes and stared at the other three women in the boat. They were all so much younger than her. They had so much to live for. They were just babies she thought. They all looked just as scared and miserable as she did. They were all hoping for a miracle and she was praying for one. She tried to trust and believe that God would see them through and they would be rescued soon. Peach was guessing that they had only been out on the water a few hours. She knew it was crucial for everyone to stay positive and encourage one another. With this in mind, she became the first one to speak up. Peach sat up in the boat in the lotus position and cleared her throat to get the other girls' attention. All three women looked her way. "I know we are all very confused and scared right now. We didn't ask to be in the situation we are in. I don't know you ladies, but I think it may help us stay positive if we at least tell each other our names and share our feelings. I think it would help us all keep clear positive minds while we wait for help. My name is Peach and I have two beautiful twin kids waiting at home for me. I also have a pretty wonderful husband also. I know they are worried sick because I was supposed to call home this morning when we arrived in Bernini. I am a believer in God. I have been praying that God sees us through this tragedy. If any of you ladies want to pray with me I welcome you," Peach said.

After Peach finished talking all the ladies stared at her but none of them spoke up. Peach just assumed they were too frightened to talk so she waited a few more seconds for one of them to speak up. No one said anything so she turned away from them. Then all of a sudden she heard the voice of one of the women. She turned around and the woman who sat with her arms crossed over her chest, spoke up. "I'm Jewel, and let me just say that I am highly pissed off that we are stranded out here in this damn ocean. It's so hot and uncomfortable out here my makeup has melted off of my face. I can't wait to get back home so my parents and I can sue the hell out of this cruise line. This is beyond ridiculous."

"My parents are very wealthy and I'm sure they are going to spend whatever it takes to bring down whoever is responsible for this nonsense. Do you know the value of the things I had to leave behind on that damn cruise ship? I spent thousands of dollars on new swimwear and clothes for this trip. I just want to get off of this damn water like yesterday because the day of reckoning is coming for whoever is responsible. I don't know about you ladies, but I am going to own this cruise line by the time I get finished," she said. Jewel was angry that she found herself in a situation such as this one. She sat in the corner of the boat with her arms across her chest, and none of the other women dared say anything to her, but they knew how she felt. They figured it was best to just let Jewel vent and leave her alone a few minutes.

They all were angry at the situation they were in, but the other girls didn't quite choose to express it the way Jewel had. Then one of the other women in the group spoke up in what was just barely a whisper. "I'm Jackie: I just want to say that I have never felt so disappointed in my life. I feel like the universe has let me down. I had so many high hopes for this trip, and now look at me stranded out here in the middle of nowhere. I should have known. My whole life has just been one big disappointment. I could care less if anyone rescued us. I don't want to go back to the states anyway. I can't go back home. I just wanted to go to Paradise. I'm okay with the fact that we may not get rescued. My life is already over anyway," Jackie said. Jackie then leaned her head over the side of the boat and stared blankly into the ocean water.

Jackie started to cry. Tear after tear fell from her eyes blending in with the ocean water. Nobody knew Jackie's painful history except her, so the other women didn't question her on why she said the things she had just shared. Peach leaned over to Jackie and started rubbing her back to try to comfort her. It was becoming obvious to all of the women that each of them was more than what met the eye. There was so much fear and anxiety, Peach thought to herself that it was going to be extremely difficult to encourage them to think positive.

Peach continued to rub Jackie's back. The girl was so young and naive. Peach wished there was more she could do to help her, but being in such a trying situation there wasn't much she could do. Peach looked at Jackie and thought to herself that she had never seen someone so young with so much sorrow and sadness in her eyes. Peach could tell just from looking at her that she had lived a hard life. After a few minutes of silence went by Peach and Jewel looked over at the other young lady in the boat. She was the only one that hadn't told them her name. Jewel looked at her and thought she saw some familiarity in her face, but she just couldn't recall where she knew her from. Jewel said, "Hey, what's your name?" In a rather shaky voice Giselle, responded.

"My name is Giselle, and I am so sorry that we are all in this terrible situation. I am trying my best to remain calm and stay positive that we will be rescued, but it's hard. I feel like I'm suffocating out here in this boat. I'm trying to think of my mother to give me strength. I don't want to die out here. I have so much to live for. I have so much more talent and music I want to share with the world!" Giselle said. "Wait!" Jewel yelled. "That's where I know you from, your music videos! You are Giselle, the R&B artist! I knew you looked familiar to me," Jewel said. "I just read an article about you on a gossip site online. I didn't know you and Chris Brown were an item. You know he still messing around with his ex. Girl you are so naive." "Excuse me!" Giselle yelled. "I don't mess around with anyone. I have never even said two words to Chris Brown. How dare you question me on that garbage under these circumstances," she continued. "That's why I don't read the garbage they put on-line. None of it is very truthful. All it does is ruins people's lives." Peach interjected. "Listen apple, or pear, or whatever your name is. I was talking to Chris Brown's girlfriend here. I didn't ask for your input on how you felt. Some of the things they post are true. They wrote an article about my parents being successful millionaires and that's absolutely true," Jewel snapped back at Peach. Jewel then rudely rolled her eyes at Peach and turned her glance back towards Giselle. Taking the cue, Giselle jumped in; "Anyway like I was saying, yes, I am a singer. I just started working on my second album, but sadly my first album could possibly be my last if I don't make it out here."

"Don't think like that honey, we have to think positive. I have faith that we will be rescued soon. We need to just remain as calm as we can. There are only us out here so we need to give each other strength to get through this. Now does anyone have anything they were able to bring with them that may be useful to our survival out here?" Peach asked. Each woman searched all of their pockets, and then visually scoured the boat. Jewel looked behind where she was sitting. She spotted a black pouch over in the corner. She wondered what could be in there. Whatever it was she was not sharing it with the other women. She didn't know about those other common women, but she was willing to do whatever it took to survive. She quickly lifted her shirt up and snapped the pouch around her waist. Then put her shirt back down over it before the ladies spotted what she was doing. The ladies turned back around and faced each other. Everyone stood empty handed. They didn't have anything except the clothes on their backs which were still damp from the waves splashing up into the boat during the night. "If they don't find us soon we are going to die out here. We have nothing, no food, and no supplies. We can't possibly last that long in these conditions," Jewel vented.

"Its okay, we will be alright. They should definitely be looking for us by now. We just have to be patient," Peach said. Every couple of minutes one of them would put their hand up to their brow to form a sun visor and scan the waters around them. Then another would do the same thing and look into the air searching for any sign of a rescue helicopter or plane. The more they searched and didn't see anything the more disappointed they became. Peach, Giselle, and Jewel sat silently in the corners of the boat and Jackie continued to sit perilously on the edge of the boat. She still didn't say anything else to the other women. She just sat gazing down into the water. It was almost like she was seeing something the other women weren't.

Peach looked over at Jackie, she was starting to really worry about the young troubled woman. They were all scared and stressed but she sensed that Jackie wasn't exactly handling the situation as well as the others. At that moment Peach decided she would keep an eye on the young girl to make sure she was alright. The hours rolled by and the sun was unmercifully blazing down on them. The women didn't have anything to protect their skin so they began to develop skin blisters from the heat. They were in agony. They were all sweating profusely from the heat. Peach had taken several anatomy and physiology classes in college so she knew how potentially dangerous this could be. They were sweating away their bodies' water supply, but they didn't have fresh drinking water to replenish it. At this rate their bodies would start to dehydrate rather quickly.

The women were parched. It had been well over a day since any of them had anything to eat or drink and they were now feeling gripping, constant hunger pains. They knew that if help didn't come soon they wouldn't survive long out on the ocean. Jewel was becoming upset and irrational from the thirst and hunger. Her tongue was dry and heavy and it was sticking to the side of her mouth. Jewel jumped up from the corner of the boat and yelled "I can't take this shit anymore, we are slowly dying out here!" she yelled. Then Jewel leaned over the edge of the boat and started drinking large palms of the ocean salt water. "No, stop Jewel!" Peach yelled. "Listen Jewel, we all very thirsty and hungry but you can't drink the ocean water. I know our situation has turned desperate but that water can shut down your organs with all the salt it has in it. It can kill you. We just have to hold on a little bit longer," Peach urged.

Jewel had a look of frustration and defeat on her face. She leaned back from the edge of the boat and went back over to the corner and sat down. Jewel wanted to cry but she didn't want to let the other women see that display of emotion from her. She didn't want to appear weak to the other women. So instead she sat with her face buried in her hands. Giselle looked over at Jewel and then quickly turned away. She understood her frustration. She felt like the situation was rapidly becoming hopeless. It was becoming harder and harder to believe that they would be rescued.

The ladies sat silently and waited. Jackie, Giselle, and Peach took their shirts off and tried to shield the sun from their faces and body but it wasn't working. The sun's heat continued to burn their skin. Jewel did not take her shirt off, she had to make sure she concealed the pouch she was hiding behind her. "This heat is ruining my skin," Jewel wined. "I'm going to need at least a week at the spa to get my skin back to health after this." Jackie raised her head up, looked at Jewel and scowled.

She was fed up with Jewel and how she threw her wealth around. She was too ignorant to even realize that she too could die out here, and the fact that she came from wealthy parents wouldn't save her. Jewel needed to be put in her place and Jackie decided at that moment she was going to be the one to do just that. Jackie looked over to Jewel and said, "Why don't you stop bragging about how much money your parents have. They can't have all that much money. They haven't sent a rescue plane to get you yet. You know some of us didn't grow up with the wealth you have. You are very ungrateful. Here you are stranded out in the middle in the ocean and all you have talked about is your parents' money. I use to always dream and fantasize I was wealthy, and that I didn't have to worry about if there was going to be food in the refrigerator when I got home from school. Then again, if I had money and had the arrogant and selfish attitude you have, I would rather stay poor."

Jewel stood up and walked over to Jackie and got right in her face. "Who the hell do you think you're talking to bum?" Peach sensed this situation could get really bad fast so she spoke up. "Ladies let's calm down." Jewel yelled back, "No, I will not calm down! I want to know who this little bum thinks she's talking to." It's not my fault I'm wealthy and she's poor. I bet she snuck on that cruise ship. It's no way she paid for a ticket like the rest of us."

Then, in an instant, Jackie lunged at Jewel knocking her down in the boat. Jackie wrapped her hands around Jewel's neck and started choking her. Giselle quickly backed up in the corner of the boat. She couldn't believe what she was seeing. These women were crazy. Peach quickly jumped into the fray and began trying to pull the women loose. "Stop it! Stop it! This is ridiculous!, Peach yelled. After a few more strong tugs on Jackie's shoulders Peach was able to pull the women loose. She quickly stood in-between the two women. Jewel backed up in the corner of the boat rubbing her neck. She looked at Jackie and pointed her finger at her, "You ever put your hands on me again bum and you won't have to worry about if you'll make it off this boat. I will wait until everybody goes to sleep and hold your head under the water until you stop breathing. Nobody puts their hands on me, especially a bum like you!"

Just then Jackie started to lunge at Jewel again, but this time Peach stopped her. Peach positioned herself between the two women. "Listen ladies this is childish. I know we are all frustrated, but fighting one another is not helping the situation. Please just calm down," Peach urged. Jackie looked at Peach and seen the look of desperation on her face, so Jackie folded her arms across her chest and backed into a neutral corner of the boat. Jewel looked over at Jackie and mouthed, "You lucky you have Mother Theresa here to watch your back."

Jewel plopped her body down in the corner of the boat, and the pouch snapped loose causing it to fall out in the open. The contents of the pouch spilled out. Among the contents was a 16ounce bottle of water. Jewel quickly reached down and grabbed it. Giselle spotted it before the other women. "What the hell is that?" she asked. Have you had that pouch hidden the entire time? Have you been selfishly hiding that from us? Jewel spoke up defending herself, "Look, I found the pouch first. It's only right that I get to keep what I want out of it," Jewel snapped.

Peach looked over at Jewel. She couldn't believe this woman was so cold-hearted. She was indeed a devil on earth. She had never met anyone in her life like Jewel. How could she keep the pouch from everyone? It could be something in there that could help them. There could be distress signaling equipment in there. "Jewel why didn't you tell anyone about the pouch you found. The right thing to do would be to bring it to everyone's attention," Peach said.

"I didn't have to tell you ladies anything, and don't even think about asking me to share this water with any of you. I found it so I'm entitled to it, all of it. Jewel quickly open the bottled of water and guzzled down half of it then threw the bottle in the ocean. "Now whoever wants it can go get it." I will not die out here on this water. I am an important wealthy member of society. My death would be devastating to my parents and the rest of the world. I'm going to do whatever it takes to survive out here. Who would my parents leave their money to if I die out here, huh? Your lives are nowhere as near important and valuable than mine. I am somebody. My name means something."

"For instance, Peach if you die out here your husband will raise your children, and eventually remarry. He will be okay after awhile. Giselle if you die, your record label will just move on to the next hottest artist they discover. In a couple of years people will hardly be playing your music. Lastly, if 'Jackie the bum' dies, who would care? She said herself she didn't care if she got rescued or not. So you see, I can't afford to not make it off of this boat."

"Jewel you sound like a crazy lunatic. Just because your parents have money, that doesn't make your life more valuable than ours. We may not have the wealth you have, but none of us want to die either" Giselle said. Just then Jewel picked up the contents that spilled out, put it back in the pouch and threw it at Peach's feet. "Quit whining Giselle. Here, you ladies can see if anything left in there can be of some help." Jackie looked up at Jewel and looked her in the eyes, "You could have shared that water with the rest of us. You just signed our death certificates. There was enough water there to at least moisten our mouths for awhile. You are a sneaky, selfish, bitch." "Call it what you want bum," Jewel said.

Peach grabbed Jackie's shoulder and pulled her towards her, because she knew if given the chance, Jackie would try to kill the girl. "Jewel, that was a very hateful thing for you to do. You have a cold, cold, heart. We are all out here suffering. If I would have found that bottle of water, I would have made sure you ladies got some before it even touched my lips. I am going to pray for your soul Jewel. I know God will see us through this difficult situation" Peach said.

"Listen Mother Theresa, I don't want to hear about your God right now. I'm tired of your preaching already. It's not helping the situation. If there was a God what would be his purpose for having us out here suffering. I know I don't deserve it. So you can keep your sermons to yourself. I don't care to hear them," Jewel said. Peach looked up at Jewel and for a split second. She felt like slapping some sense in the young girl. She knew that would only make a tense situation worse, so she just shook her head and kept her mouth shut. Peach picked up the pouch and examined its contents. She wasn't feeling very optimistic about what she found inside. There laid out in front of her was a compass, several bandages, and tape and gauze. She opened the pouch a little wider, and shook it more thoroughly, but she didn't come up with anything more than what she already had in front of her. Peach thought this was insane. She asked herself out loud "How could there not be any rockets or flares in here. Don't they routinely check these lifeboats to make sure it's equipped with proper distress equipment?" They were in the middle of nowhere moving east according to the compass. Peach picked up the items and put them back in the pouch. She inhaled deeply and blew it out. She slowly scooted back over into the corner of the boat. She looked around at the other women. They were all under a lot of stress mentally and physically. She could only pray that help would come soon. They needed a miracle and they needed it now. The ladies quietly sat in the corners of the boat until the day slowly started dwindling away. The ladies finally felt relief when the sun began to set, but at the same time they were overwhelmed with disappointment because they realized they would be out on the water another miserable, dark night. As the sun set and the moon rose into the sky, down went the hope of being rescued that day.

It once again became virtually pitch black. The only light they had was coming from the moon shimmering over the ocean. They couldn't help but feel that no one was really looking for them. No one spoke, because no one had to. They were all thinking and feeling the same hopelessness. None of them had thought that they would be out there a second night. They were expecting to be rescued right away, and here they were going into another night. Jewel was in one corner of the boat with her face buried in her shirt. She was trying to force herself to go to sleep, so she could get away from this real life nightmare. Giselle had her back turned to the rest of the women. She was so emotionally drained; she didn't know how long she could mentally hold it together. She was literally was on the verge of losing control.

Peach was in another corner of the boat, praying. She prayed for God to help her and the other women. She prayed that they would have the will and the strength to hold on. She prayed they would courageously face whatever plan he had set in motion for them. She prayed for her children and her husband. She knew they must be worried sick about her. She wanted to stay positive and believe that help would arrive, but if it was God's will to take her now, she prayed for peace of mind and comfort for her family. Lastly, she said a special prayer for Jackie. Peach felt that the young girl was troubled. She just seemed so hopeless. Peach thought Jackie had such sadness in her eyes and was willing to bet it had been there long before this tragedy. Peach was really worried about Jackie so she silently vowed to keep an eye on her no matter what the outcome may be.

After Peach, Giselle, and Jewel fell asleep, Jackie sat up and looked around at the other women. She felt so bad for them, except Jewel. She had no remorse for Jewel, even if they were going to die out there. Jackie's body was suffering more so than the other ladies. No one knew that Jackie had not eaten one day prior to the cruise ship leaving the port. She was so excited and nervous about leaving, that food was the last thing on her mind. Then her first evening on the cruise ship she decided to go down to the dinner buffet for supper. Everything looked appetizing but she had no appetite. Her plan was to go back to her room and eat the muffin she had brought with her from the diner. She was so exhausted by the time she got back to her room, she climbed into her bed and fell fast asleep. She had not actually slept in a bed in days, and the one in her room was so nice and comfortable she fell asleep and forgot all about eating the muffin. Two hours into her deep sleep she was awakened by a crewmember instructing her to come to the upper deck to be evacuated. So in actuality, she had not eaten in three days, and it was starting to have its effects on her.

She wasn't a stranger to being hungry. She sometimes went all day without eating as a kid. Her mother would feed her when she remembered, or when she felt like it. Those hunger pangs were nothing like what she was experiencing now. She had never been this hungry in her life. It felt like her stomach was being ripped apart from the inside out. It was constant and unstoppable, and she found herself losing control. The hunger was overpowering her, making it hard for her to think clearly. It was starting to make her delusional. She started to see things that weren't there. At one point she thought she spotted her father out in the ocean swimming towards her. He was screaming the words "You can't run away from me Jackie! Wherever you go I will follow you!"

The delusion caused her to shake in fear. She quickly closed her eyes so tight her eyeballs hurt. She held her eyes closed waiting for her father to grab her at any second. But when she opened her eyes a few seconds later, the image of her father had disappeared. Once she came to the realization, that she was hallucinating, she decided to try and get some sleep. She curled up into a fetal position in the corner of the boat and went to sleep.

A little after 3:00 in the morning Jackie awoke from a deep sleep. She sat up and looked around at the other women. They all appeared to still be sleeping. She looked around and still she couldn't see any-thing on the horizon. It appeared that they were still the only ones out on the ocean. Jackie was feeling a little dizzy and confused. She thought how the hunger and dehydration was really starting to make her feel bad. She leaned over the side of the boat to splash a little water on her face to wake herself up a little bit.

What she saw in the reflection of the water left her speechless. There, down in the water, was a vision of her paradise. It was like a movie clip playing out for her to see. There she was lying out on the beach in her pink two-piece bathing suit. She looked happy. Her face showed peacefulness and contentment. She could hear the sound of the coconut palm trees blowing in the wind. She could see herself pick up a handful of the warm sand, and let it run through her fin-gers. She loved the feeling.

Jackie realized she could be having delusional visions, like she had with her father a few hours before. But this one was different, it looked so real.

She wanted so badly to be there in her paradise. She had dreamed about it for so long. Jackie continued looking down in the water at the vision. She saw a woman come over to her in a pretty multi-colored swimsuit and offered her a drink in a coconut. Jackie watched herself reach out to grab the beverage. What she didn't realize was that she was reaching out physically in reality. She reached out until half of her body was hanging over the boat and, in an instant, she fell over the side of the boat into the warm ocean water.

The impact of the water hitting her body shocked Jackie back into reality. Immediately she became terrified. She started screaming for help, splashing and throwing her arms around violently. She had never learned to swim. She knew at that moment if she couldn't keep herself afloat long enough to holler for help from the other women, she would die out in the ocean alone.

Something had caused Peach to awaken during the night. She sat up and slowly looked around at the other women. She noticed that Jewel and Giselle were asleep but Jackie was not. She seemed to be looking down at something down in the water. Peach didn't quite understand what she was doing. She was staring down in the water earlier but this time she was actually leaning over the side. Peach sat and watched Jackie a few seconds wondering what was down in the water holding the young girl's attention.

Peach then saw Jackie leaning over the side of the boat with her arm stretched out like she was reaching for something. "What the heck is she doing?" Peach thought to herself. She was leaning over too far. "Jackie!" Peach yelled at her, but it was too late. Then in an instant, she saw Jackie fall over the side of the boat into the water. Peach heard Jackie instantly yell for help and she sprang into action. She yelled for Jewel and Giselle to wake up as she started to take her clothes off to go in after Jackie. She yelled loudly "Jewel, Giselle, wake up! Help me! Jackie has fallen into the water! I can't see where she is, I need your help!" Peach begged.

The two women woke up and realized what was going on. Giselle immediately started panicking. Jewel sat with her arms crossed. She didn't seem to care that Jackie had fallen overboard. Peach was out of her pants and shirt. She took a deep breath and jumped in the water. She momentarily had the wind knocked from her as her body reacted to hitting the water. She went under a few feet and then resurfaced looking around for Jackie. She called out to Jackie. "Yell Jackie! Its dark and I can't see you!" Peach urged. Peach looked around and then she heard Jackie's voice about ten feet away. "Help me please, I can't swim! I'm going to drown. I can't keep my self above water! Please don't let me die!" Jackie begged.

"Keep kicking your feet Jackie, I'm looking for you. I'm coming, hold on baby girl," Peach shouted. Peach and Giselle looked around for Jackie frantically, but it was hard to tell where she was in the water. Peach continued to swim around and look for Jackie while Giselle continued to search the water. Then Peach couldn't hear Jackie screams anymore. Her heart dropped as she prayed silently to herself, "Please God, don't let this young girl die out here. Don't take her yet lord."

Peach was getting tired herself and her lungs were burning but she was not going to give up looking for Jackie just yet.

Peach took another deep breath and then dove back under the water to look for Jackie. She searched around frantically but she couldn't see her. Peach swam back to the surface to take another breath when she heard Giselle yell, "Peach, I think she is over there! I see bubbles over there!" Peach quickly swam in the direction in which Giselle was pointing. She took a deep breath and dove back under the water again. She immediately spotted Jackie's limp body under the water's surface. Peach quickly grabbed Jackie and brought her head above water. She knew Jackie had swallowed too much water. She knew it was just a matter of seconds before it would be too late to save her.

Peach herself was weak and physically exhausted from swimming around. The fact that she had not had any food or water for two days made it worse. She knew she had to find strength from somewhere to swim with Jackie on her back to the boat.

Then she thought about her babies back home. This young girl was still a baby. She had yet to really experience what good life had to offer. Peach knew if it was one of her kids out there in the water, she would want someone to do whatever it took to save them. With that in mind Peach summoned the last ounce of strength she had and struggled back to the boat with Jackie on her back. Once she reached the boat she yelled, "Help me get her in the boat fast! She swallowed too much water. I have to perform CPR!"

Giselle reached down to help Peach and Jackie. Jewel still sat with her arms crossed. She had made up her mind that she wasn't doing anything to help Jackie. "She should have never put her hands on me," she mumbled. With Peach pushing and Giselle pulling the ladies were able to get Jackie's body back over into the boat. Then Peach pulled herself up over the edge with help from Giselle. They laid Jackie's body flat in the bottom of the boat and Peach started chest compressions. Every 15 seconds she would stop and check for a pulse. The first time she didn't find one so she continued the compressions followed by blowing air into her lungs. Jewel stood in the corner of the boat watching Peach do CPR on Jackie, while Giselle was kneeling on the side of Jackie's body holding her hand. Giselle had started to cry uncontrollably. She didn't know the young lady, but she didn't want her to die.

"Please God bring her back to us. Come on Jackie baby, come back to us," Peach repeated to herself out loud. Just then the women heard a faint sound in the distance. They all knew that familiar sound. It was the sound of a helicopter. They couldn't believe someone was still looking for them and had finally found them. Peach continued to perform CPR on Jackie, and she yelled to Jewel and Giselle, "Please yell! Scream! Wave your clothes in the air! Do something to get their attention!" Peach once again checked Jackie for a pulse and there was none. She was becoming exhausted from the chest compressions, but she wasn't ready to give up. She continued on. She didn't want to give up hope that Jackie would make it. She had been performing CPR for two minutes and had not found a pulse. She hoped and prayed this was a rescue helicopter looking for them. Giselle and Jewel stood in the boat yelling and screaming the best they could with their voices becoming hoarse from dehydration. They were waving their hands in the air desperately trying to get the attention of the people in the helicopter. They all hoped this was the end of their nightmare as the sound of the rescue copter grew louder and louder.

......................To be continued

Made in the USA
San Bernardino, CA
10 April 2016